The Gobi
Lost Treasure Beyond a

Cedric Daurio

Bluthund Community Collecion

THE GOBI CODEX- LOST TREASURE BEYON A FLEEING HORIZON

The Bluthund Community Collection

Copyright © 2024 by Oscar Luis Rigiroli

All rights reserved. This book or any portion thereof may not be reproduced or used in any manner whatsoever without the express written permission of the publisher except for the use of brief quotations in a book review.

This is a work of fiction. Names, characters, businesses, places, events and incidents are either the products of the author's imagination or used in a fictitious manner. Any resemblance to actual persons, living or dead, or actual events is purely coincidental.

Dramatis personæ

Werner Scheimberg: Archaeologist sent to Tibet in 1938. by the Thule Society.
Wolfram von Eichenberg: Young Scheimberg´s assistant.
Dorje: Old Buddhist lama in Tibet, Wolfram tutor.
Tara: Tibetan priestess. Wolfram mistress.
Martín Colombo: Argentine young man visiting New York
Dennis Colombo: Martín's distant relative, resident in New York.
Deborah Liberman: Dennis's girlfriend.
Selma Liberman: Deborah´s Sister.
Jack Berglund: Member of the Bluthund Community, specialist in runes.
Lakshmi Dhawan: Woman born in India, member of the FBI.
Anila Ragnarsson: Lakshmi´s daughter.
Aman Bodniev: Siberian shaman.
Roman Ungern von Sternberg: Russian military. Warlord active in Mongolia in the period 1917-1921.
Batbayar: Mongolian expedition guide
Tsetseg: Mysterious Mongolian woman, member of the expedition.
Hans Wildau: Dark character at the service of an unknown organization.
Gerda Schmiddel: Secretary of an enigmatic character called Direktor.

Dr.W. Richardson: Master of the Bluthund Community in New York.

Jerome Watkins: master of ceremonies at Bluthund events.

Dr. Dieter von Eichemberg: Scholar specialist in Eastern and Western esotericism.

Madame Nadia Swarowska: Member of the Bluthund Management Committee.

Suzuki Taro: Member of the Bluthund Management Committee.

M. Garland: Agent of the British MI6.

Sir David Osborne: Former head of MI6

Yeshe: Tibetan guide.

Liu Daiyu: Captain of the Chinese People's Army.

Liu Hung: Chinese Colonel. Daiyu's father.

Prologue

1938 -Tibet
Wolfram von Eichenberg carefully lifted the broad flat stone, helped by two of the Tibetan bearers. The remains of sand that had covered it for countless centuries slid down the sides. Under the stone, objects of vague contours could be glimpsed with clear tonalities that varied from red to yellow to blue. With infinite care Werner Scheimberg, the senior archaeologist sent to the expedition by the Thule Society, began brushing the sand and mineral particles outward, exposing an evidently organic substrate. Wolfram watched the scientist's methodical procedures with anxiety. Suddenly Scheimberg exclaimed.

" No doubt it is a mummy." And added immediately " We have to treat these remains with caution because they can disintegrate between our fingers. In addition, the location of each element that we find can give us valuable indications of their way of life." He was evidently exalted and removed the young man from the excavation with a little brusqueness.

After three hours of work, the find was free of detritus and ready for visual inspection. It was the remains of a middle-aged man, about six feet tall, covered by what were undoubtedly traces of a cloth of various colors that covered the body.

"This is amazing." Said Scheimberg. "It's absolutely out of context."

" What do you mean Werner?" Replied von Eichenberg

"This man was not an ancestor of the Tibetans or of any Mongol race. Look at the height and shape of the body. It is typically Aryan."

Werner's heart started beating strongly. That finding could be a first confirmation of the theories they had come to test in the Gobi desert.

It was the year 1938. The explorer Ernst Schäffer had organized his third expedition to the East sponsored by the German *Ahnenerbe* and under the auspices of the Tibetan government. The aim was to test some theories enunciated by the official esoterists of the Third Reich and the Führer himself, according to which the cradle of the Aryan race was in an Asian region covered afterwards by the Gobi desert and since then disappeared from the face of the Earth, but that still existed in an immense complex of subterranean cities, a thesis that was related to the oriental myths of Agartha and Shambala. This was in turn related to the theories of the hollow Earth in vogue in Nazi Germany

Von Eichenberg and Scheimberg were part of that expedition, accompanied by an entourage of bearers and guides, as well as a Tibetan seer who, the Germans supposed, had in addition to his formal guiding mission the function of spying on them for the government of that country. Scheimberg had been one of the companions of the Swedish explorer Sven Hedin on his excursions in the East, with archaeological and to some extent esoteric purposes. Von Eichenberg was just a young man with an eagerness for adventure and exoticism, without any relevant scientific qualifications

After a day of meticulous cleaning of the mummified body, Werner Scheimberg was in a position to make a verdict.

"It is certainly not one of the precursors of the Indo-European race trumpeted by our theories, but one of its members in its own right. His whole aspect, his face admirably preserved by the dryness of the sands, the reddish tint of his hair and beard and the woolen fabric of his clothing strongly remind the primitive Celtic tribes. It looks like a primitive Scottish warrior."

"Tonight I'll get in touch with von Schirach by radio." Replied Wolfram. "Have you prepared the report you want to convey to him by then?"

The young man, obviously not too impressed by the find turned around and left. From an aristocratic family, he had never been enthusiastic about Nazi racial theories, and to his eyes Hitler and his henchmen deserved a certain disdain. The theses on the hollow Earth and the submerged cities seemed absurd to him and therefore also the same purpose of the mission; however, he took good care not to express those ideas in public. From the East, it was another thing that had him dazzled.

Upon returning to Jiayaguan, a city on the edge of Tibet at the foot of the Qilian Mountains, both men went to the house where they were staying, Scheimberg was writing his report on his old typewriter while Eichenberg went to get a shower and change his clothes. When he finished, the young man passed by the room where his partner was working.

"Werner, I'm going out now. At twenty hours I'll return and call von Schirach."

"I suppose you're going to visit that priestess who has trapped you between her legs." The comment was answered with silence.

Wolfram went to the Buddhist temple led by an old lama named Dorje, who had taken him as a kind of disciple, though coming from a very different culture; the old monk was excited because he had an attentive student who absorbed his teachings like a sponge.

That day Dorje explained to his disciple the deceptive nature of concrete matter, in reality manifestation of a divine energy that must be channeled inside our minds and bodies to free us from our carnal attachments, our desires and ties. In a persuasive tone he told Wolfram that each being is a manifestation of that energy and that he already possesses everything necessary for his spiritual sustenance that only needed to be recognized and nourished.

As usual after the lesson Wolfram remained absorpt under the influence of the accumulation of thoughts and sensations for more than an hour in absolute silence. Finally he regained his usual state of consciousness and left the cabin, noticing only then that Dorje had already left.

In one of the corridors he met one of the novice monks, and asked him.

" Chodak, can I visit Tara today?"

" I think she's anxiously waiting for you." Replied the young monk.

The answer, in another context would have been paradoxical. Tara was Chodak's sister as well as an important Tantric priestess; Chodak did not ignore the motivation of the German's interest in his sister, and he knew that he was reciprocated by her. But while in our Western culture the relations between the sexes are tinged with a halo of sin and suspicion, in the aforementioned branch of Buddhism sex has high and even sacred connotations.

Tara and Wolfram were sitting in the woman's bed. They knew that no one would come to interrupt them so they proceeded with infinite calm, avoiding any anxiety.

The priestess was wrapped in veils that the man was drawing back in a parsimonious way, dominating all animal instincts. The desire had to acquire sublimated forms before freeing itself. Tara explained the three sacred purposes of sex, each of them elevated and sublime: reproduction, pleasure and liberation of the soul.

She was guiding the young man through the ritual including the previous purification steps. Once they had finished with the preparations both were seated on the bed facing each other with their legs entwined. Guided by the priestess, they united in an ecstatic embrace, a precursor of reciprocal caresses that lasted an eternity. Finally came the moment of intimate union of both lovers, in which each of them dissolved into the other, and both into the cosmic consciousness. At that moment the Kundalini serpent would rise, achieving the fusion of Shiva and Shakti, the masculine and feminine principles. The ritual concluded with penetration and ejaculation, followed by a prolonged period of silent union.

Wolfram retired from the room invaded by a physical, psychic and spiritual ecstasy incomparable with any of his previous experiences while the woman reclined on the bed and again covered her body with her veils.

The young man took a long detour to return to the old house where he was staying. He felt himself floating among clouds, in a state he had never known before and wished that it would last as long as possible before confronting Scheimberg and his archaeological skills. Suddenly he consulted his watch and realized that only fifteen minutes were missing for the agreed time for the radio call to von Schirach, kind of coordinator of all the teams then working in East Asia; for that reason he hurried to avoid being late for the appointment.

"Ah! Finally you come." Said Werner. "What a smile, have you been transported back to the fifth paradise?"

Wolfram did not answer and simply put the radio equipment in conditions, and at the scheduled time, established the contact.

The conversation between Scheimberg and von Schirach lasted about forty minutes. Although Wolfram had somewhat moved away he perceived that the tone of the verbal exchange was harsh and that Scheimberg was limited to listening most of the time. When the radio contact was finished, Wolfram looked at his partner and asked.

"So, how did it go?"

Scheimberg's face pre-announced what the answer would be. He was disturbed and his gesture showed discouragement and disenchantment.

"He basically told me we did not come to the end of the world to look for the skeleton of a Scotsman. What interests the *Ahnenerbe* and the Thule Society is a kind of missing link between the precursors that they suppose inhabited in this area and the current Aryans. I do not know what they want, a kind of Atlantean."

" Which is no news to you."

"The one we have made is an important archaeological finding." said Scheimberg obviously dejected. "It shows that the Indo-European expansion to this area took place much earlier than assumed. The other Nazi expectations are simple chimeras."

Then he looked at Wolfram in alarm. If that phrase had been heard by other members of the expedition, among whom there were several SS informants, that slip could have had serious consequences for Scheimberg. Then he sighed in relief. Although Wolfram had never expressed himself freely on the subject, he was aware of the young man's skepticism about the racial theories of Nazism. Scheimberg's mood changed from dejection to a hint of envy. At least Wolfram had found in the Gobi Desert something that gave his life a purpose, even if it was between the legs of a sacred dancer.

" What shall we do now?" Asked the young man.

"We go back to the excavation, in particular to the neighboring grotto that we discarded the first time."

The cavern was long and sinuous and had different branches. The men split and Wolfram went inside with a torch in a tunnel that had its ground covered by sand. In one of the bends he suddenly stumbled over a partially covered rock that caused him to roll overland. The torch had happily not turned off and he picked it up while he was still on his knees. When he was trying to get back on his feet a reflex caught his attention. A bright object had been exposed as a consequence of his fall. He pushed aside the sand that still partially covered it and saw that it was a golden disc about two inches in diameter. Wolfram picked the object up with a handkerchief and examined it in the uncertain light of the torch. Clearly it was a sort of roughly circular gold medal with certain incisions that attracted him. When he observed them more closely, he jumped astonished. While on the obverse some broken stripes could be letters of some forgotten alphabet, on the reverse the German managed to clearly see a swastika although its edges were somewhat worn out perhaps by the abrasion of the sand.

At that moment Scheimberg appeared silently from the shadows behind him. The young man showed him the piece found and noticed the excitement in the face of his comrade.

Both carefully proceeded to remove the sand from the vicinity of the site where the disc had been unearthed, and it was then that they emerged in the light of the Scheimberg lantern.

The bones, obviously cranial, were too thick to be fully human.

The two men looked at each other in silence.

New York City

Current Times

Chapter 1

Once the process in the Migration sector was completed, he walked to the Baggage Claim area where the passengers swarmed waiting for their suitcases to appear on the conveyor belt that was assigned to their flight.

SINCE THE ONLY LUGGAGE the young man carried was a large backpack and a small wheeled suitcase that he had placed in Buenos Aires in the luggage rack above the seats, he passed by the area on his way to the exit. In total, the process of entering the United States had taken three quarters of an hour, mostly due to the long queue that foreigners had to do before Migrations. Upon leaving the huge lobby mixed with disoriented travelers of all races and nationalities mixed with internal transport agents in search of customers to take them to the various hotels in the city, the boy smiled. New York was offering to him its usual nervous and busy face. The memories of his long previous stay flocked to his memory, and all the smells and flavors of the city flooded his senses. Resolutely he went to the area of the buses that connect the Airport with the center of the city where he would pick one of them to take him close to his destination. The rest of the trip he would do by subway or walking. As far as he remembered, the Gramercy Park area was a residential and quiet district and he wondered what his distant relative would be doing in such an elegant area.

His heart was jubilant. Immediately after his twenty-third birthday party at home in Buenos Aires, Martín Colombo returned to New York after four years of absence; in his mind this city was the portal of all kinds of adventures and experiences. At the end of the previous year he had taken his final exams at the National Technological University where he graduated as an industrial engineer and before joining the small systems consultancy firm set up by his brother Román, Martín had agreed with him and his parents that he would dedicate the following period to travel the planet and then enter fully into the adult world of formal work, in a kind of *sui generis* sabbatical year. To that end he had little money but at least he had a contact that according to his father would give him shelter and whom he could help in his tasks in exchange for a small remuneration; the nature of the tasks and activities were unknown to Martín at that time but in reality he did not care at all as long as they gave him time and freedom to travel the city and actually around the country.

The contact was a distant relative named Dennis belonging to a branch of the Colombo family that had migrated to the United States at the same time his grandfather settled in Argentina. Martín's father had met members of that branch who had remained in Italy when he had visited the small town of Inveruno in the province of Milan. When Martín had previously traveled to New York, his father had not yet been to Inveruno and did not know of the existence of that relative, so they had not met him then. When both tried to find out what Dennis was doing, the answers had been vague, so they presumed that the Colombo relatives living in Italy really did not know.

Martín pressed the doorbell of the apartment and while he waited for the answer, he looked around the peaceful neighborhood with its houses built obviously at different times but with a sober and elegant aspect and it was only then that he noticed the relatively few people who passed by at that time, an experience so different from the usual feverish rhythm in New York. He was lost in those thoughts when the electric bell rang and a male voice spoke to him from apartment 3C, where he had called.

"I'm Martín Colombo." said the boy in still hesitant English.

"Come in." The speaker said succinctly in a husky voice. "The elevators are at the end of the corridor."

Dennis Colombo turned out to be a corpulent man in his forties. At that moment he was unshaven and looked a bit disheveled, but when he saw Martín he smiled and turned away from the door to allow him access.

The living room was large and shallow but tastefully furnished and it seemed to Martín that behind that aspect there was a feminine hand. Several books were open and scattered about what was obviously the dining room table, and at his side were scrawled some notepad blocks. At one end of the room, next to a window was a work table with two computers, a printer and other technological devices.

"Come, I'll show now you what your room will be." Dennis said showing him the way through a short corridor. The room was small but cozy and had a single ample bed, a wardrobe with much room for the few belongings the boy was carrying and a light table. Also near the window was a small work table; the place looked clean and tidy. Martín left the suitcase and the backpack on the bed.

"So, what do you think?"

"Very good indeed, this is all I need and more than what I have in my own home."

"Come." Dennis said again . "Let's have a coffee."

At the moment they were both going back to the living room and the owner of the house was heading towards what was evidently the kitchen, key noises were heard coming from the apartment door.

"It's Deborah, my girlfriend." explained Dennis; when he saw the young man's doubtful gesture, he then added immediately.

"Don't worry, Debbie does not live here, she has her own apartment near Central Park, but she has a key to my house and we spend a lot of time together."

"It is fine by me. I do not plan spending much time inside the apartment; I want to tour the city."

Deborah Liberman entered the apartment and hung her coat from some hooks placed for that purpose next to the door. Martín looked at her admiringly and without saying a word. In her late thirties, tall, blonde, with intensely blue eyes, harmonious features with a nose of slightly Semitic profile, the woman was beautiful and no doubt by her elegant looks she made an impact with her mere presence. Deborah was dressed in a blue coat and skirts of unquestionable quality that made even an ignorant absolute of the fashion like Martín realize that it was brand clothing. The contrast with the worn jeans and the pullover somewhat deformed by the use of the young newcomer made him feel somewhat out of place; this feeling was, however, relativized by looking sideways at Dennis, who was even more modestly attired.

"Martín, let me introduce Debbie." said Dennis, taking the boy out of his stupor." Debbie, this is Martín.

Following the custom of his country the young man approached to kiss the woman on the cheek, but she anticipated extending his hand.

"Sit at the table." Added the homeowner. I´m already coming with coffee."

Martín sat at one end of the table. As he watched forward he felt that the woman's beautiful eyes were resting on him, which increased his sense of discomfort, but when he looked straight ahead at her he realized that she was looking at him smiling but in silence. At that moment Dennis returned with the steaming coffee pot. Debbie hurriedly pulled out some cups and dishes from a cupboard and placed them on the table, so the man filled them. Just then the woman's voice was heard and in spite of his lack of practice in the language Martín immediately perceived that she spoke educated English.

"So you're the lost relative of South America." The tone was friendly.

"Argentina." The boy specified.

"Argentina." She repeated calmly." I have already been told that in your country you are proud people."

"I ... I really did not want ..."

"And who told you?" Dennis interrupted, addressing the woman with the hidden purpose of removing his relative from the embarrassment.

"Students from other Latin American countries." She answered.

"Debbie is a professor at an art academy." explained Dennis.

"You have handsome relatives in Argentina." The woman commented. "No doubt Selma would like to meet Martín."

"Selma is her younger sister." explained Dennis once again.

" Tall, with light color eyes and hair. It's not the idea we have of the Italians in New York." added the woman.

"The Colombo family comes from the north of Italy." Dennis had taken charge of giving explanations of everything that was said.

"I want to hear you speak." Debbie said now addressing Martín." Do you speak English? Tell me about your life."

Encouraged by the good vibes of his two interlocutors, the young man began to tell them his short biography, interrupted every so often by questions from the two Americans, who obviously had little information about his country.

"So you've gone skiing last winter." The woman said. "One associates Latin America with tropical climates."

"The south is very cold. You know ... Patagonia, Tierra del Fuego ... Antarctica is not far away."

As he spoke, Martín was growing more comfortable speaking English and the evening with the exchange of information continued for several hours, until Dennis said.

"It's time to have dinner."

Martín discreetly looked at his watch. Debbie noticed and expressed.

" It's half past seven and p.m. What time do you usually have dinner in your country?"

"Hardly before nine of the night, but I'm hungry, today I ate little because of the trip."

"I'm going to order the food." Dennis resolved. "You can choose Italian, Chinese or Indian. It's the repertoire we have in the area."

"None of that!" Debbie said standing up. "Today I'll cook. We're going to have Martín try a New York dinner."

"Is there such a thing?" Dennis asked jocularly. "Well, you know better than I what supplies you will find in the refrigerator."

Chapter 2

As he was returning from his visit to The Cloisters and on the long bus trip Martín meditated on the first week passed since his arrival in New York. The young man had remained true to his avowed intention to know the remarkable places he had not visited in his previous stay in the city with his parents. The next day he had planned to visit the Ground Zero and the remarkable buildings that had been built around the emblematic place.

But it was not tourist thoughts that haunted his mind in the last two days. Once his youthful desire to know had had a beginning of satisfaction, the commitment he had acquired with his relative and that justified, at least formally, the hospitality that Dennis offered by admitting him into his home, came to the fore. This commitment, although never expressed explicitly, consisted in helping the host in his work and studies. However, at that time Martín had to admit to himself that he had no idea what these tasks consisted of. While he was watching the succession of urban landscapes through the bus window, the young man took the decision to directly address the issue with his distant cousin because he already knew that Dennis would never ask him for help in exchange for lodging.

At that moment the vehicle made one of its stops and a black girl with very graceful features and a body of spectacular curves ascended; the boy's eyes could not detach from her behinds until his sight suddenly crossed with that of an old lady, also black, which looked at him with an air that Martín interpreted as reproach. His thoughts changed quickly and he remembered that hat night he was invited to dine with Dennis and Deborah in the woman's apartment, and that the meeting would be attended by Selma, whom he did not know yet but about whom his relative had communicated through winks and smiles that shared the beauty of her sister. This meeting had generated expectation in the boy, who had been for a while without female company.

"Are you ready? We must leave now to arrive at seven. Dennis' voice came from his bedroom.

"I'm almost ready." The boy hastened to finish his task; Dennis had lent him an electric iron and he had taken his best shirt out of the suitcase where it had been until his arrival and was ironing it on the bed. He picked it up and judged the general appearance of the garment, which seemed satisfactory to him so that he proceeded to put it on immediately.

"Here I'm." said Martín entering the room while putting on his jacket.

"Let's go then." Dennis opened the apartment door and they both left quickly.

The building where Deborah lived was elegant and everything in it breathed an air of high status, increased when they entered the luxurious lobby once the woman remotely opened the door to them.

Debbie looked resplendent as always, a fact that intrigued Martín, who despite being an attractive young man barely managed to look presentable. Upon entering the apartment, the boy could see that it was furnished and decorated in a very sober fashion, despite having all the amenities. The stripped aspect was achieved by avoiding the accumulation of unnecessary objects that every house ends up putting together. The painting of the interior and the curtains managed to maintain a luminosity that was in keeping with the minimalist impact it caused.

AT THAT MOMENT A GIRL emerged from what was evidently the door of one of the interior rooms. Also blond and light-eyed, she had a rather thin frame and features that clearly denoted the kinship with Deborah. As it used to happen to him with everything concerning the latter Martín was affected by the young woman and momentarily he felt that he could barely articulate words. As had happened previously, Debbie came to his aid.

"Martín, this beauty is my sister Selma. According to my father she´ the family´s diamond, what incidentally, makes me feel jealous." The tone was however jocular.

Once again the boy did not know how to proceed, which was saved this time by the same Selma who extended her hand.

"Debbie tells me that in your country people kiss on the cheek at the very moment you know each other." She said in an inquisitive tone. "Do you consider that a hygienic custom?"

"Well ... well, I ... I do not know, it's the habit."

Once again Debbie saved her guest from her bewilderment. This time she burst into a loud laugh.

"Well Martín, you should know that my sister is that frontal and that she usually proceeds in this way to make all the boys feel insecure... particularly those she likes."

This time it was Selma's turn to blush while exclaiming.

"Oh Debbie! I wonder if you are my sister or my enemy. With what right do you interpret my actions in your own way?" However, she could not prevent her tone from sounding falsely offended.

Debbie served the dessert after a menu consisting of dishes cooked by her along with others bought in some delivery but that formed a homogeneous group. The talk had been referred to circumstantial issues such as the menu itself or the vicinity of the woman's apartment. At the time of the coffee, Selma, who had contributed relatively little to the dialogue, moved her chair back as if to gain some perspective from it, focused her eyes on Martín and asked.

"You are tonight novelty." The tone was determined and somewhat inquisitive but cordial. However it lit some alarms in the boy who until then was in a comfort zone with the inconsequential talk.

"Tell us something about you." The girl continued.

" Something like what? What would you like to know?"

" Actually still being relatives I do not know much about you either." added unexpectedly Dennis. " I support Selma's request. Tell us something about Buenos Aires, about your family, your studies, and your friends."

It was Martín's turn to move his chair away from the table and reflect on what he was going to say.

"Well, I hope my poor English does not betray me."

"Your English is better than many New Yorkers´." Debbie's tone was exhilarating as she showed that she, too, was curious about her guest.

" The one who came to Argentina was my great-grandfather Paolo Colombo ..." The boy found himself talking with a calm unexpected a minute before. " ... who ended up marrying the daughter of a Basque immigrant ..."

The exposition lasted over ten minutes without interruption from the other diners.

"... and I suppose that on my return to my country I will start working with my brother Román in his small company."

" So this trip is a kind of transition time before being initiated into the world of adults." Concluded Debbie.

" A century ago the upper middle class youngsters longed for a trip to the jungles of Africa before entering a family business." The home owner continued reflexively." Today you have chosen the jungle of New York to quench your thirst for adventure. Tell me, what has guided your choice? Why New York?"

" Well ... I suppose having a relative, although distant as Dennis, had some influence on the choice."

Selma's voice and tone surprised everyone.

"Along the chosen site you have made a decision that requires at least some courage. I envy you! It's more than I've done, although I'm your same age."

"That statement is amazing to me though I see you almost daily." Debbie exclaimed sincerely. "So you too feel thirst for adventure?"

"What about it? Do you think I should not?"" Selma was a little angry. " Why, because of my sex?"

"No, no, no." The sister cut in. " Do not get me wrong. I love that you have your own projects and even hidden ones. It's just that I had no idea of them."

"Bah! Devoirs of young bourgeois who have their economic problems solved from the cradle. If you had to earn a living you would have other hidden desires." Dennis's tone was realistic, with no grudges.

"Oh! Shut up, proletarian." Debbie exclaimed as she was sitting next to her boyfriend, giving him a push after which both burst into laughter . Then he turned to his sister and said tenderly.

"I want you to tell me more about those unsatisfied cravings. As your older sister I have not the right but the duty to know them."

"I cannot be more precise, I do not know how to define this ... craving as you call it. I have always played the role of a rich girl."

"There are worse roles than that." Dennis noted with his usual irony.

"... and I would like to experience something different."

"And would you be willing to take some risks?" Asked suddenly her sister.

"Yeah, sure."

Suddenly Debbie and Dennis exchanged glances, which did not escape the scrutiny of Martín who was following the scene without uttering a word. A moment of dense silence followed the dialogue. Deborah made an almost imperceptible nod with her head to her boyfriend, who was also intercepted by the Argentinean. Suddenly Dennis stood up with the gesture of a man who has made a decision. His face had abandoned the funny gesture that usually had and appeared serious.

"Well, Martín had anticipated before that he wants to work with me in my ... in our work." He said looking at Debbie, who again nodded. "And now you Selma say you want to shake off your drowsiness and accept risks."

He made a silence that lasted a few moments and then continued.

"We will give course to those concerns." New look at Deborah." For this we will meet Saturday morning in my apartment. By then Debbie and I will have a proposal prepared. Is at 10 in the morning okay for everybody?"

Chapter 3

"Have you ever heard the name Bluthund?" asked Dennis in a supposedly casual tone, as he came back from the kitchen with a steaming coffee pot.

"Not ever." Selma and Martín answered in unison. The latter closed his mouth allowing the young woman to continue speaking, in an attitude that would repeat itself over time.

"Should we have heard?" Asked the girl.

"Not really." The homeowner's response was paradoxical. "In fact, I am relieved to know that the secret is well guarded."

At that moment the door of the apartment opened and Deborah entered with a package of cookies that she had bought at a nearby store. After that she set to listen to the conversation, refraining from making any comments. Once Debbie had sat down at the table with the others Selma again asked a question to Dennis, though now her tone had a hint of youthful impatience.

"Will you tell us once and for all what it is that Blood ... whatever?"

"Bluthund. It's a German word that means bloodhound." said Debbie intervening for the first time in the conversation; then she looked questioningly at her boyfriend.

"No, no. You go on." Said Dennis said as he poured coffee.

"Can you please end this secrecy and explain what we are talking about?" Selma did not have much patience left.

"Bluthund is an informal group, without statutes but with a governing body, which was formed in social networks but then took a more hermetic and even somewhat secret status. It includes researchers from the most diverse disciplines, who often do not know each other personally, and yet collaborate through the Internet in the resolution of cases and problems of difficult handling. It has no financial support from governments or any type of organizations. They have certain ... "particularities"."

"What do you mean?" The conversation had been reduced to a dialogue between the two sisters.

"To the research methods."

There was a moment of silence.

"So? Or will we have to get every word out of you with a corkscrew?" Selma's hostility was only apparent.

"It's hard for us to talk about this issue with people who do not belong to the group."

"But we have just asked them to come today to introduce them to the topic." said Dennis. "Will you speak or shall I speak?"

"You're right. Well...there it goes." Debbie took a breath and began her explanation.

"The methods that Bluthund uses in its research come from both the positive sciences and from "alternative knowledge branches"."

"What do you mean by alternative?" It was the first time that Martín actively participated.

"Precisely not based on those positive sciences, but on traditional knowledge, in arcane of different cultures."

"Arcane?" Selma frowned at the question.

"Yes, hidden, mysterious things, secrets that come from the depths of time and have been exhumed by modern researchers."

"It sounds like esotericism. Am I wrong?" Asked the Argentinean.

"Perhaps, but they are not attributed a sacred value but a practical one. They are taken as methods that cannot be explained in the light of science and yet help solve problems."

"Problems? What kind of problems?" Selma had regained the lead in the interrogation. Her voice always sounded inquisitorial.

"Unexplained, bizarre, intriguing themes, often from the past but with current repercussions. Political, cultural or police facts, or the mixture of all that. The themes are proposed by the various members of Bluthund anywhere in the world and the group sets out to investigate it, with no time frames."

Selma was going to ask another question but was unexpectedly interrupted by Martín, the young man had leaned his body forward, in a position of maximum attention.

"And do you have success stories in your research?"

"You'd be surprised." The answer came from Dennis, relieved to find that his relative had been caught by the subject. "Tell me, what do you think of what you've heard so far?"

"All this has an air of…. I do not know how to define it…tell me, are you working on a specific topic now?"

" Yes, in fact we have a devilishly complicated case between hands. " The owner of the house smiled when seeing that the conversation had finally caught Martín´s interest.

"Tell us what it is about." The change in the modulation of Selma's voice showed that she too had been swept away by the halo of mystery that had first seduced Martín.

They had finished the coffee. Dennis got up from his chair and said to his companions.

"Let's go to my office … that is, to the living room. I have things I want to show you."

The large desk that Dennis used to work was covered as usual with open books and various papers. A desktop computer and two notebooks flickered as a result of their energy saving systems. The man brought chairs of the dining room for all and once they had sat down he inquired.

"I'm going to ask you another bizarre question. Have you heard of Agartha or Shambala?

The faces of the two youngsters showed again perplexity. Selma was the first to react.

"Shambala, it sounds like a rock band or pop song."

Dennis erupted in a loud laugh; Debbie looked at him defiantly and said reproachfully.

" Do not laugh at them, they are two young people who have a known world limited to their generation, just as it happened to us at their age"

"No, no, sorry. I did not mean to make fun of you, but the observation took me by surprise."

"Well, are you going to explain what you're talking about or not?" Now it was Martín who looked impatient.

Dennis was absolutely amused at seeing the interest aroused by his question. He leaned back in his chair and began his explanation.

" Both are terms that come from esotericism but from two different cultural areas. Agartha is more linked to the theosophy of the West while Shambala is a recurrent myth in various Eastern traditions. However, both have some common elements."

"For example?"

"The two terms refer to mythical kingdoms in the East, hidden for human beings, although some of their inhabitants may have sporadic or permanent contact with ordinary men and women. I'm going to ask Debbie to tell us about Agartha."

The woman thought for a moment how to begin her presentation.

"Who in the 19th century gave a more or less complete reference to Agartha was Madame Helena Blavatsky, the Russian creator of Theosophy, allegedly based on much earlier traditions. Later both the name Agartha and the concept were used by twentieth century occultists such as Roerich and Ossendowski. Basically Agartha is related to the belief that the planet Earth is hollow, that there are cities and kingdoms of superhuman races or at least beings more evolved than humans who avoid contact with them. These subterranean worlds communicate with the terrestrial surface by means of secret entrances hidden in the summits of the mountains, in the Desert of Gobi, and even under the oceans. The beings that inhabit those great subterranean galleries are not only more developed than the humans in the scientific terrain but also in their sensorial powers and especially in their moral concepts. They went to live inside the Earth a long time ago when they realized that the Universal Flood was about to happen, so they could survive it."

" All this is incredible!" exclaimed Martín. "On what grounds dot they base such audacious affirmations?"

" Right. What evidence do they have to prove what you are saying?" added Selma.

Seeing the agitation produced by the myth among the listeners Debbie decided to continue with caution.

"The presumed evidences are prophecies and affirmations made by clairvoyants and collected and amplified by occultists from various schools."

Seeing gestures of skepticism in the faces of the young people Dennis thought it appropriate to add an annotation.

" Do not forget that the fact that Bluthund collects these testimonies does not imply that its members share the theories of those occultists. We must not forget that many ancient religions were able to foresee eclipses and other astronomical events with great precision even though they believed that the stars were gods. The Babylonians are a good example of that."

" That is to say, although these theories are based on absolutely erroneous beliefs they can nevertheless provide useful tools for the analysis of problems." completed Deborah.

"Granted. Keep talking." Selma asked her sister.

"The sites proposed as portals to that underground world vary according to the authors and range from Siberia, the Andes Mountain Range and the Amazon rainforest, but the most frequently mentioned is the Gobi Desert, in Central Asia. Beneath its sands and stones allegedly inhabit the most advanced race of these subterranean beings. That explains why it was the site chosen by the Nazi esotericists in their searches."

"Nazis? What role do they play in all this?" Selma's face showed disgust.

Chapter 4

"Yes Selma." Dennis answered immediately. "You cannot explain the phenomenon of Nazism just for economic or political reasons. All his detestable racist surface ideology was based on esoteric beliefs communicated to the followers by some of their leaders, especially Hitler himself, his subordinates Hess, Rosenberg and above all Heinrich Himmler, the all-powerful creator of the SS and concentration camps. All of them used the services of seers and in some way were shaping the Nazi ideology on occult bases. Its central nucleus was generated by a secret organization called Thule Society, created by a man called von Sebottendorff before the assumption of power by the Nazis. They believed that under the Gobi Desert lay the keys to the birth of the Aryan race and that their origins had to be sought there."

"You must know that between 1931 and 1938 the Nazis sent two pseudo-scientific expeditions to Tibet to look for traces of those origins in the dispersed populations in the Himalayas." Debbie paused." Those expeditions were under the command of a biologist named Ernst Schäffer and in their activities they performed thousands of anthropometric measurements to Tibetan villagers, claiming that the leaders of that people had Aryan genetic traits. Himmler himself believed he was reincarnation of a remote Saxon king named Heinrich.

" How is it possible that such absurd beliefs have developed in highly educated and scientific societies such as the Germany of that time?"

" It's a good question."Deborah answered." But I'm afraid I do not have a good answer."

Martín, who had been silent until then suddenly got up and snapped.

"I have listened carefully to all your explanations but I have a question. The group that you belong to ... Bluthund, are you interested in all this subject of Agartha, Shambala and Nazi esoterism by pure... let's say... academic curiosity? Or is there a more specific motive moving you?"

Dennis, obviously satisfied by his relative's sensible question, signaled to his girlfriend that he would take charge of the answer.

" Actually, for both. All these themes harmonize perfectly with the "alternative knowledge" that we handle in Bluthund, and we have already stumbled upon the Nazi myths in the past."At that moment he paused.

"... But it is also true that the fact that we are now dealing with these issues obeys a specific and very material issue. A theme that has attracted the interest of some of our members."

"What is it?" Selma made again her voice heard.

"We still do not have all the information, and just next weekend we have organized a meeting with one of our colleagues who has investigated this issue and proposed it to Bluthund as a work area. This person will update us on the details. His name is Jack Berglund, one of those who has acted in the area of Nazi mythology in the past."

" You never mentioned that name to me." Selma said to her sister. "Who is this Jack?"

"An American runologist. He lives here in New York City."

"Runologist?"

"Specialist in Scandinavian runes. He just got in touch with the Nazi theme because they used runes in their mythology. For example, the fearsome SS formations took their name from a rune called Sowilo."

" And why just next weekend?" Martín's impatience was the true reflection of the interest that the issue had awakened him

"Because Jack must take certain precautions to move around."

"What happens? Has he got outstanding accounts with justice?" Selma's question was logical.

"No. His accounts with the justice have already been settled. They were issues related to his professional activity. The enemies Jack must take care of now are of a different nature, more hidden and more fearsome. Therefore, special precautions must be taken."

Selma and Martín looked at each other somewhat bewildered.

" For that reason we will prepare a picnic or the coming weekend." Dennis continued.

"Really?"

"Yes."

The Bear Mountain State Park is located in the Rockland County, in a mountainous area of New York State placed on the west bank of the Hudson River. The zone includes lacustrine landscapes, streams and groves suitable for picnics.

Dennis silently guided a rented car and drove silently so he could concentrate on the many curves on the road and determine the location chosen for the meeting.

"Have you been here before?" asked Debbie.

" Yes, a couple of years ago. I hope I will remember the curve in which we have to leave the road and park.

"So far I've seen see very few cars and few people on this site." said Martín.

"The weather is very variable and today's forecast indicates rain. It is not a day that many would choose for a picnic." answered Deborah.

"Debbie, I think there's some information about Jack that Selma and Martín should know before we meet him. I want to concentrate in driving the car. Why don't you tell them?"

"All right."The woman responded, taking a few moments to sort out her ideas." As we told you, Jack was imprisoned for his participation in an incident related to Bluthund, and for reasons that we never knew was released shortly afterwards. Those who moved their influences to set him free tried to manipulate him but he did not live up to their purposes and these people persecuted him ever since. Jack had a girlfriend named Lakshmi Dhawan, a woman born in India and a FBI member, who took part in many of the events that happened then but when Jack was convicted she ended up marrying another academic member of Bluthund, an Icelander called Ingo Ragnarsson, with whom she had a daughter, Alina, who today must be about six years old. Eventually Lakshmi and Ingo divorced and when Jack was set free he tried to go back with her. There is no doubt that Lakshmi and Jack always loved each other but circumstances played against them. We do not know what happened next."

"There it is!" Dennis interrupted. "I recognize the place."

He drove the car to a dense grove on one of the edges where they all descended. As noon time approached, Debbie and Dennis carried several baskets with the food supplies they had brought.

"Now I know that the picnic plan was serious." Exclaimed ironically Selma.

"Secret plans or not we have to eat." was the simple answer.

" What now?" asked Martín.

"Now we eat and we wait for Jack to appear."

"Aren´t we meeting at a fixed hour?"

"Approximately at noon."

They had already had lunch and had collected all the debris to dispose of it somewhere outside the park. The two sisters had left the place to walk around the site in order to reach a nearby stream; the place was idyllic despite the threatening sky. The three men had been sitting on the floor, talking about banal issues.

Debbie and Selma walked along the descending path that led to the watercourse. In a moment Selma was startled by the agitation of branches of nearby bushes behind which a diffuse shadow appeared; the young woman looked scared at her sister, who had also perceived the movement and was looking expectantly in that direction.

"Hello Deborah." The voice was close and produced a relaxing effect on the woman, who ran to a man who had emerged from the vegetation and embraced him, to the perplexity of her sister.

"Oh Jack! it´s been so long."

They hurriedly walked towards the place where the men were. Martín lay on his back on the grass talking to Dennis and when he heard a noise he turned around and found himself alone. His relative was running towards the approaching group. The Argentinean looked at the newcomer, a bearded redhead giant that brought a number of Viking characters to his mind.

Dennis had embraced the man and it was evident that both and Deborah shared an old affection.

Dennis made the introductions with a lump in the throat so that his girlfriend had to complete it.

<Well, so this is the famous Jack. I have to grant that he has an imposing presence.> thought somewhat bewildered Martín; then he looked at Selma and noticed that the girl was also a little shocked.

Since the newcomer had not eaten the picnickers shared with him the lunch they had brought while they were sipping coffee. The talk was monopolized by Debbie, Dennis and Jack Berglund and revolved around shared experiences and what happened after their separation, which according to their estimates had taken place three years earlier.

Once the conversation about memories subsided, Jack asked his old friends.

"Well, are these the guys that are going to accompany us in this new stage?"

"Yes," Dennis answered. "As we have explained before, both are related to Debbie and me and are absolutely trustworthy."

Berglund leaned against the trunk of a tree, and despite his previous stressful appearance was now relaxed. Debbie reflected that in his random life the man probably did not have many chances to be safe among friends. In an impulsive gesture she asked.

"Dime Jack, how are your things, you know, the personal ones?"

The man looked at Selma and Martín and then at the woman.

"As Dennis told you, you can speak in front of them." Added Deborah, anticipating her friend's doubts.

" As you may know, I told Lakshmi that I want to have a second chance with her. The problem is that I have to hide myself permanently and being together would limit her and the girl's activities and on the other side would be incompatible with her FBI membership, so we should content ourselves with meeting in a clandestine way, as you and me have found today."

The air with which Jack answered was sad and melancholic and clearly showed his state of mind. To throw his friend off his depression Dennis thought it was time to talk about the subject that had brought them together. Without mediating any introduction, he said.

" Jack, tell us about Agartha."

The aforementioned turned around in his resting position in the trunk while looking for the tip of the ball to begin his narration.

"Have you ever heard about Aman Bodniev?"

" Never."

"Bodniev is a Siberian shaman who lives in a lost cabin in the taiga, serving as a healer to the few inhabitants of Yakuta origin who live scattered in those desolate plains. He has demonstrated his gifts of clairvoyant in the past with notable successes in the search for lost people in the tundra, objects and in the prediction of events. He has always shied away from putting his talent at the service of Russian governments, but from time to time he introduces some new... let's call it intuition to the small group of people who know him."

"And has he manifested any of those ... visions now?" Dennis's tone showed a clear skepticism.

"Yes, on a subject that has baffled many explorers and adventurers of all stripes for almost a century."

"What is it about?"

Jack again answered with a question.

"Is the name Baron Roman Ungern von Sternberg familiar to you?"

"No. We do not know anything about him either."

" Well, in this case this is going to be a long story." Jack settled back on the floor.

" When the communists took power in Russia in 1917, it took them years to extend it to all the immense territory that was to constitute the USSR. Groups of aristocrats and people linked to the Tsarist past revolted for a long time and confronted the Bolsheviks with arms. One of the most important was Admiral Alexander Vasilyevich Kolchak, a hero of the Russo-Japanese War and the First World War, when he commanded the Tsarist Imperial Fleet. Kolchak established a state independent of the Bolsheviks based in Omsk, until 1920 when he was betrayed and executed by the Communists. His troops, consisting of white Russians and Poles made a desperate withdrawal pursued by the Bolsheviks through thousands of miles of Russian territory, Mongolia, China and Tibet trying to reach colonial

India. It was on arriving in Mongolia that they found our character, Baron von Ungern."

"Who was he?" asked Martín, his attention once again evidently captured by the narration.

" Baron von Ungern Sternberg, possibly born in the Baltic countries, had two conflicting personal characteristics. On the one hand, he was a military man with a great strategic capacity and a fanatical supporter of Russian nationalism. On the other hand he was a mystic very knowledgeable of Buddhism and Tibetan Lamaism, and apparently considered himself a reincarnation of the Mongol god of war. He went from being a general in the anti-Bolshevik army in the civil war in Russia I just told you about to a true warlord who took control of Mongolia commanding his Asian Cavalry Division, wresting that country from the Chinese. That division was a formidable nomad army with great mobility and firepower. Ungern was a monarchist who wished to restore the Romanovs in Russia under the power of a Grand Duke and at the same time reestablish the power of a certain Bogd Khan in Mongolia after ousting the Chinese. It is said of him that he wanted to restore the empire of Genghis Khan in Asia."

"Is everything you're telling us true?" Inquired Selma, whose youthful mind had also been trapped by the epic story Jack was telling.

"Yes indeed, although it's not too well known because the Soviets have hidden it.

" And how does the story go on?" urged Martín, while Debbie smiled at the attention of the audience achieved by her old friend, who continued his story.

"In 1921 von Ungern commanded an invasion of Eastern Siberia with an army formed by Russians and Mongols, but was eventually defeated, captured and shot and this was the end of his story ... and the beginning of the legend of his treasure."

"WHAT TREASURE?" MARTÍN'S reaction was instantaneous.

"In his raids Baron Ungern, who was a bloody and unscrupulous individual, looted the riches of the cities he had conquered and according to the stories of those who knew him, he had collected a treasure of a great quantity of gold and silver, and numerous precious stones of great value. His purpose was not only personal enrichment but primarily to put those funds at the service of his monarchical restoration project."

" Do you know what happened to the treasure?"

"According to the legend, before the advance of the Red Army, von Ungern tried to have it carried to a safe place out of the country and for that purpose he sent it with a strong contingent of his troops but they could not cross the border and buried the treasure in the steppes of eastern Mongolia and then scattered. Thus began the myth of the treasure of the "Crazy Baron" and although many have sought it, nobody could find it until now."

After his long narrative Jack looked tired and hoarse, so he took a breath. After a while and proving that not only young people had been hooked on the story Dennis inquired.

"And how does your Siberian shaman enter this story?"

THE GOBI CODEX- LOST TREASURE BEYON A FLEEING HORIZON

Chapter 5

"That is the real news."Jack replied." It seems that he has seen in his visions a party of Russian and Mongols riders crossing the steppe and stopping in one place, deliberate there and start digging and then deposit their cargo in the hole they had opened in the bed of sand and stones. Finally, after smoothing the terrain and making certain marks, they returned along the road they had come through.

"And can the Siberian recognize the site?" asked Dennis.

"Yes, for certain mountainous formations on the horizon and the marks left on the ground."

"And that vision ... was it not produced by vodka?" Debbie's question actually represented a general doubt.

"The Siberian shamans do not act because of the influence of alcohol but of certain herbs that they burn in their sessions."

"Hallucinogens?"

"In all likelihood, yes. What is not an obstacle for Bodniev having a history of findings that statistically cannot come from chance."

"Has he indicated the area of the presumed treasure?"

" In general terms yes, but he must be present at the moment of the search to recognize the site using his methods."

"What methods are those?" Debbie insisted on her skepticism.

"The man is also a rabdomant."

" Those who use a Y-shaped tree branch to find water? There are people like that in Argentina." added Martín

" Yes, although I do not know what instrument he actually uses. They usually have pendulums of some kind, often very primitive devices."

A silence extended for several minutes while his five interlocutors processed the consequences of the narration made by Jack.

"Well, what's Bluthund's plan now?" asked Dennis.

"To organize an expedition to the area in question, in the border between Mongolia and China. They are looking for resources to finance it, government permits to work in both countries in excavations and related tasks under an archaeological pretext, and finally find volunteers within the organization to carry them out." Jack looked at his companions and continued.

"The question is if we can count on you."

The statement remained on the air while the group remained silent. Finally Dennis took the responsibility of giving a transitory response.

" Let us discuss this between us. We will contact you when we have made a decision. How will we do it?"

"As I already explained, we are looking with Lakshmi to be able to live without endangering her or the girl. I hope to have news soon. Call her, anyway I'll keep you updated."

At that moment, the sky darkened and a cold rain began to fall that in a few instants turned into hail. Jack got up and covered himself in his hooded waterproof jacket.

"Now I must go."

"You cannot leave in the middle of this storm." Dennis said pointing to the lightnings in the sky. "Come with us and wait in the car until it is over."

"No, thanks, I'll be fine. I am already used to fighting with harsh climate conditions in the open air." The man embraced Deborah and Dennis and greeted Selma and Martín; then without another word he walked towards the forest and into the grove. A hailstorm of medium-sized stones fell on the five companions who hastily picked up the tablecloth and the items they had used at the picnic and ran across the short distance to the car, locking themselves immediately in it, waiting to let the storm pass before heading back.

"What will happen to Jack in the middle of this storm!" Debbie exclaimed with a hint of anguish in her voice.

"Let's have faith in his resources to fight in adverse media." answered Dennis. "He has survived many setbacks in his life ... and yet he continues to look for new challenges."

Since she was visualizing him on the television screen of the device, when Martín rang the doorbell of his relative's apartment he heard almost immediately Deborah's voice that opened the door without asking him to identify himself. She told him at once.

"Come in. We are all here already."

While the elevator was taking him to his relative's flat, Martín mentally reviewed the latest events. The previous night he had hardly been able to sleep because of the excitement of the decision he had just made. He was fully aware that he was getting ready to start an adventure as he had never had in his life, and that most of his friends and companions of his age could not dream of. Travel to the frozen deserts of Mongolia, located almost at the antipodes of his own country in the company of a group of explorers belonging to an informal group whose binder was constituted by the management of disciplines other than the sciences and commonly accepted techniques, with the purpose to meet a Siberian shaman who would guide them in the search for a treasure of a legendary adventurer who had seized Mongolia for a failed project of monarchical restoration in the middle of the Eurasian continent. It was difficult for the young man to size up the challenge before him.

Martín was not unaware that the project was full of uncertainty and dangers, especially because the areas to which they were traveling were populated by tribes of ways of life and governed by political systems very different from what constituted his experience.

The elevator finally reached the indicated floor and the young man crossed the short corridor and pressed the bell of the apartment. His soul and mind were filled with joy and anxiety. Debbie opened the door.

"So you agree to come with us?" asked Dennis in a somewhat formal manner."

"Yes."

The man approached and gave him a hug that squeezed his bones. Martín was though more surprised by the kisses given on his cheeks by Debbie and Selma; it seemed to him that his acceptance had triggered a kind of initiation ceremony to some sort of Hermetic society, although in truth he did not have much information about it. The contact with the soft skin of the women however was pleasant and reminded him of certain experiences that had become somewhat distant.

Dennis and his girlfriend had prepared in the woman´s notebook a check list of topics that needed to be addressed before they could leave the US. Everyone sat around the computer and made comments while Debbie read the items.

" ... then, who is going to take over the task of finding out the requirements to obtain Chinese visas?"

Selma raised a hand.

"Remember to find out if those visas will allow us to move freely through the country hinterland, including the Chinese Inner Mongolia and Tibet.

"Okay."

" Who will do the same for the visa of the Republic of Mongolia?

"All right. I'll do it." Dennis said." The first thing is to know if there is a Mongol consulate in New York.

"Yes. It's on 77th Street." said Martín after consulting his cell phone.

"Now that I think about it." added Dennis, addressing his family member. "Have you asked permission for your family in Buenos Aires to travel to the Far East?"

"I have not asked permission but I have informed my parents. As long as they do not have to finance the trip, they can not oppose it."

"And what about you?" The man reiterated the question referring to Selma.

"Mom is quite nervous, but the fact that Debbie comes with us will reassure her ... eventually."

"I will talk to Mom." Said the older sister." You are already of legal age, she can not oppose."

"What about the equipment, tents, sleeping bags, mountain equipment? ..." continued listing Debbie.

"Can´t we rent it, be it here or in China?" asked Selma.

"No. We must have our own equipment."

Answered Dennis.

"I have already asked my family to send me all my Patagonian trekking equipment from Buenos Aires." Martín added.

" Do you have mountains in Argentina? I only knew about the pampas." Selma confessed her geographical confusion.

"The highest mountains outside the Himalayas are in the Andes, exactly on the border between Argentina and Chile."

The afternoon continued with the distribution of tasks that seemed endless. The feeling that the following week would be extremely busy spread among the expedition members.

Desert of Gobi

Chapter 6

The trip from New York City to Ulaanbaatar (Ulan Bator), the capital of the Republic of Mongolia had lasted a total of 18 hours, slightly longer than the established time, due to a snow storm that had delayed the departure from the Moscow airport. The two flights had been carried out on aircrafts of Aeroflot, the Russian airline. The second part, performed on a smaller aircraft, had been tiring, so when arriving at the Genghis Khan Airport in Ulaanbaatar they were exhausted. On the bus trip to the city and the hotel where they would stay for two days, both Selma and Martín fell asleep.

When they all woke up at noon the next day, the prolonged fast caused them to devour their breakfast and go to a neighboring inn to eat again. At the hotel they helped them obtain tickets on the Transmongolian Railway, which actually complemented the route of the famous Trans-Siberian Railway in Mongolian territory, on a total trip that stretches from Russia to China. The crossing on Mongolian soil follows the old Tea Route that entered the Celestial Empire.

THE GOBI CODEX- LOST TREASUREBEYON A FLEEING HORIZON

THE TRAIN JOURNEY CONTINUES to Beijing, although Zamyn Uud is the last station where passengers arrive on the Chinese-Mongolian border. The panorama is both picturesque and monotonous due to the aridity of the Mongolian landscape, where the only attractive visual element are the *yurts*, the traditional transportable dwellings of the Mongols and other peoples of Central Asia, made up of a network of woods arranged on a circular floor, forming a cylinder with a higher in the center. This structure is then covered with canvas and woolen fabrics, and sometimes with straw, which allows the users to add or remove layers according to the season of the year and thus withstand the harsh Mongolian winters. This type of housing, easy to disassemble and carry, is an essential element to the nomadic lifestyle of many of the Mongolian tribes even today. As it was said, their geometric designs and often bright colors were the only factor of distraction of the trip.

The long train ran through the immense steppe at high speed and once the attraction for the landscape was exhausted, the four travelers went to lunch at the picturesque dining car of the convoy, a spacious and comfortable place with wooden coatings of geometric designs and with upholstered seats with Mongol motifs.

After a few dozen miles the route began to gain altitude with a significant slope that lasted a couple of hours and once reached the point of maximum altitude began a descent in the middle of a winding path that produced vertigo to sensitive passengers and at the same time it offered attractive panoramic views.

From then on, the route entered the Gobi desert, one of the largest and most arid of the planet. It is surrounded by the Altai Mountains and the Mongolian steppes to the north, the Tibetan plateau to the southwest and the Chinese plains to the southeast.

Finally the train arrived at the station called Chojr, a former air base during the Soviet period, located in the middle of the Gobi Desert. In that place the travelers got off the train and rushed inside the station to escape the intense cold of the outside environment. In that place they had to wait to be picked up by the local organizers of the trip. Several hours passed without major events which began to cause a certain boredom mainly to the younger members.

"How does our trip continue from here?" asked Martín. In fact, the plan they were following was a mystery for the two youngsters and had not been made explicit until then.

"For reasons of confidentiality, the entire project is being handled with a great deal of secrecy." answered Dennis. "As far as I know, Jack Berglund will join us on this site, because for his safety he had to travel in a way that I ignore and that no doubt he will explain to us. I hope Jack knows more details of the successive steps. He is the person in contact with the members of Bluthund who organize and finance this entire expedition."

Another couple of hours passed without alternatives and this time also Dennis had fallen asleep along with the young people on the uncomfortable banks of the station. Everyone was awakened by the festive cries of Deborah, who was approaching a glass door of the station and hugging a newcomer. As he was covered by a heavy Russian coat with furs, one could scarcely see his face, although by his height and physique they soon discovered that it was Berglund, so they all came out to greet him.

"I finally left the United States through the Canadian border, and once in Toronto I also took a flight from Aeroflot to Moscow. From there my trip was similar to yours."

" Do you know how our itinerary continues from here?"

" Only partially. Now we must wait at this station to be joined by the Siberian seer I told you about in New York. As he arrives we must all go to a hotel in this city where we already have reservations and tomorrow we will meet the man who will be our guide, a Mongol whose name I do not remember though I have written it down."

Waiting at the desolate Chojr station was undoubtedly the most tedious stretch of the trip up to that point mainly due to the absence of activities to carry out, so travelers were dozing most of the time while trying to protect themselves from the cold through the blankets they carried in their luggage. At about 11 p.m. Dennis, the only one who was awake shook each of his companions and managed to wake them up.

"He's arrived and now is entering the station." He whispered in Debbie's ear.

"Who? The Russian?"

"Yes, Bodniev."

The character that had actually made his entry into the expanded space of the station was impressive. Although not so tall as Jack

Berglund, his physique was nevertheless more massive, which was enhanced by the thick Russian wool coat with fur collar and a classic conical cap, also made of furs. His features were clearly Eastern showing an influx of the various ethnic groups of Eastern Siberia; his beard was bushy, long and gray. In spite of its volume the man moved with agility and went without doubting towards the group of five travelers, really the only occupants of the station at that hour.

"Jack Berglund?" He asked.

"Yes, it's me." answered the aforementioned standing up.

"He speaks English." Selma said in a low voice that obvious relief.

"Yes." answered her sister. "Do not let yourself be guided by appearances. In another life, decades ago, he was a professor of physics at the State University of Irkutsk. Since that time he stayed connected with Bluthund."

Jack and the newcomer approached the remaining members of the group who stood up. The former made the presentations.

"Welcome to the group." answered Debbie." How should we call you?"

"My first name is Aman. You can call me that." answered Bodniev with a heavy Russian accent.

He left a kind of bag made also with skins that he used as a backpack and sat on one of the station benches.

"I've walked all afternoon." He excused himself.

His presence demanded respect and the others did not dare to ask him from where or how he had traveled. However, the conversation progressively evolved and Jack sought to deftly channel it towards the activities to be developed. At one point he said.

"We have reservations made for everyone in a hotel at the village. There we can leave our belongings and have dinner. Then we will spend the night in that place. We can chat at dinner."

Only when they left the station did they notice how dark it was, and what the night meant in the Gobi Desert. The cold was intense, a wind blew dragging particles of sand and forced them to walk inclined and covering their faces; they all looked at Aman to see how he behaved before the hostile nature, in the belief that he was the one to be imitated.

Selma raised her eyes to the dark sky with the new moon. Seeing the huge amount of stars that studded her the girl could not help but utter a moan and instinctively touched Martín's arm in order to share the show with him. The boy smiled, pleased with the gesture and Selma hung on his arm to overcome the resistance of the wind.

Chapter 7

Sitting in a small room on the ground floor of the hotel where a smoking samovar was the only source of heat in the room, the conversation was directed towards the experiences of the Siberian shaman related to the purpose of the expedition. With his usual naivety, Jack asked directly.

"Aman, what should we look for? Where can we find it? How shall we know that we have found it once we do?"

Bodniev shifted uneasily in the chair he had sat on, which was otherwise too small for his body. He looked at his companions, still narrowing his slanted eyes that formed into two lines, gave a snort and began to speak in a slow voice. His English was heavy but clear and the coherent speech showed a reflection behind him.

"I am afraid that I will not be able to answer all your questions to your satisfaction, not because of any desire to hide where we are going, since I understand the concern you surely have about our immediate destiny and the questions about the dangers that we can face in our search . The truth is that I ignore most of the answers and that the source of my visions does not follow a rational path. They are not formal thoughts spun like beads in a necklace, nor logical deductions from clear premises, but rather blinks, flashes that refer to issues that I can sometimes associate with facts of reality and other times not."

"And in this case?" asked Debbie with a certain urgency. A little regretful of her impulse she looked at her boyfriend who secretly made a gesture that she interpreted as not losing patience. The Russian continued with his unshakable voice.

"The theme of the "Bloody Baron" as Ungern von Sternberg is known in these places for the blood he shed and the treasure of the Mongols that he ordered to be protected and whose trail was lost, is an issue that comes to my mind in a recurring way, so I know perfectly well when one of those flashes that appears in my visions refers to those issues. That's the way it happened before I made contact with Bluthund, so I know that my current sights refer to Ungern and his treasure."

With slow movements Bodniev removed a paper from his bag and began to unfold it carefully, revealing a wide map with annotations written in the Cyrillic alphabet. Then he went to a nearby table and placed the map on it, which occupied it almost completely. Then he extracted from the same bag a strange artifact, consisting of a metal spindle with a sharp point and a cord at the opposite end.

"This is a radiesthesia pendulum, like those used by dowsers, to locate springs of water, metal veins ... and so they say, treasures." Dennis clarified in a low voice to a distrustful Deborah.

The Russian turned around facing his companions and scrutinized them patiently, then said softly to Selma.

"You, girl, would you like to come over please?"

The girl looked a little fearful at her sister and then at Dennis, who gave her an almost imperceptible nod with his head. She took several steps to reach the table and looked at the inscrutable map, while the others approached her in what represented a moral support. Bodniev offered her the pendulum and once again the girl hesitated.

"Take it, it will not bite you." Said Jack, who had remained silent until then. Selma took the instrument from the opposite end of the spindle, unfolding the string about fifty centimeters long.

"Now pass it slowly over the map, sweeping from left to right and vice versa." indicated the Siberian.

The girl began to perform the task that had been entrusted to her starting at her discretion from the upper left to the right and returning in the opposite direction to reach the other end of the map.

"Very well, do it very slowly." Said the Russian in a deep voice.

Once she had gained confidence Selma moved the instrument through the chart neatly with gentle movements. Debbie whispered in her boyfriend's ear.

" All this is ridiculous; I do not know what you expect. We are losing our time."

"Shhh." It was the only answer.

Selma had already passed the pendulum for more than half of the map and felt that her arm was getting tired.

"You can change arm if you want, continuing from the same point." said Bodniev.

The young woman did so and continued her slow scanning with her left hand. A smile enigmatically appeared on her lips and suddenly the pendulum produced a strong and unexpected swing surprising everyone, starting with Selma. From there the movement continued with a gentle swing while the Siberian said in a firm voice.

"Stop there." Then he turned around and looked at all present.

"The girl has detected the same place on the map that I found in my repeated tests."

"Can I mark the place on the map? " Martín asked Bodniev.

"Do it."

The young man took out a thin pencil from a kind of school tool bag he carried and approached. Then he asked Selma.

" Lower the tip a little more, until it is almost in contact with the paper, so as not to make parallax errors."

The young woman did so and Martín made an X on the paper

"How far is that point from our current location?" Dennis asked the Russian.

"Some 755 miles south-southwest.

"Can I do some checks?" Martín asked again.

"Of course."

Then the boy took out of the bag of surprises a short plastic rule with a transporter.

"First I will orient the map." He said while activating the application of a precision compass on his cell phone. He turned the map on the table until it was oriented according to the compass rose, divided into 32 directions. Then he asked the Russian, indicating a segment at the bottom of the map, written in Russian.

" Is this the scale?"

"Yes."

" And where is the station in which we are now?"

Bodniev marked a point written in Russian.

"Let's see what the engineer says." Dennis expressed in Debbie's ear.

Martín measured the distance in centimeters between both points. Then he marked the icon of the calculator on the cell phone and entered some values.

"The distance is approximately 750 miles indeed." He said. "And the direction is, also very roughly, south-southwest."

"Is this the direction in which according to the previously existing data the treasure should be found?" Jack asked.

"Decidedly not." replied the Russian." Everyone has looked for it some 70 miles further west."

"And do you have any idea of where this discrepancy can originate?" asked Dennis.

Bodniev turned and looked at him meditatively.

"In one of my visions, of those flashes I was talking about, the men sent by Baron Ungern suffered the onslaught of one of the tremendous winds that blow in the Gobi Desert, with speeds of up to 170 miles per hour, which produce the blasting of soils, a fact that prevents agriculture in its entirety. Travelers are bombarded by sand and particles of all sizes. In my vision the Russians and Mongols were completely disoriented so it is no wonder that they have given wrong locations of the place where they deposited the treasure."

Jack had been intrigued by the whole recent episode so he approached the Siberian and asked him in a low voice.

"Have you chosen Selma at random or did you have any reason to select her?"

Bodniev nodded and replied enigmatically.

"The girl has powers of which she is not yet aware, I can easily sense it. It is a treasure that must be recognized and developed."

"What would have happened if any of the rest of us had used in pendulum?"

"It would not have moved when going through that point."

" How do you explain that?"

"The sensitivity is not in the instrument but in who uses it. The real sensor is the dowser, not the device."

" Does that mean that Selma is ... a clairvoyant?"

"It means that it is equipped to be. To become one, she must make an effort, under the proper guidance."

The American withdrew in silence thinking about the unexpected confession of the shaman and meditating how he could transmit it to his friends.

They had gathered at a table with meat dishes purchased at the hotel. At an offer from Jack the Russian answered.

"No, thanks, I have not tried vodka for decades."

"Well, we'll settle for cold tea..."

The snack was silent, since everyone had a delayed appetite. After a while, and as if to prove that this hunger had been satisfied, Dennis asked.

"Well, what happens now?"

"Didn't Bluthund's members give you directions?" Bodniev answered with another question.

" I have requested them before leaving for here." added Jack. "But in the end what they answered is that you would give us more details."

"Well, during the course of this morning we will be picked up by some Mongols in three all-terrain vehicles, suitable for the desert that we have to cross. I do not know how many people will come."

"What will be the function of these people?" Debbie intervened in the conversation.

"Varied. They will serve as guarantors to the Mongolian or Chinese authorities we might meet, they will be interpreters, guides in the desert and ... escorts."

"Escorts?" Selma asked with a frown. "Like guardians?"

"That's right. They will also help us with the excavations that we will eventually have to do."

" Will they be armed?" inquired Martín.

"Of course."

"Do we need armed guards? " Selma insisted.

"The territories we are going to cover are far from any town, security forces or source of any formal authority. Often there are attacks and looting of the caravans or isolated travelers who cross these solitudes, and many disappear without leaving traces. If the means of transportation in the desert is taken away from you, it is very unlikely that you will be able to survive hunger, thirst and nighttime cold."

"Decidedly I prefer to be protected by armed guards ... as long as they are trustworthy." Martín argued sensibly.

"I do not know them personally." Bodniev finally said. "But I do trust the people who recommended them to me."

A silence spread among the members of the group, who were undoubtedly internalizing for the first time the reality of the dangers that awaited them.

Nothing happened during that afternoon and just in the mid-morning of the following day three vehicles of unreliable appearance appeared in the corner of the hotel. One of them was a dilapidated Russian truck in which they would load the necessary equipment to establish camps, the implements to carry out excavations, the provisions and any type of load that they could obtain in their searches; it was manned by two Mongolian drivers and carried into the box four other fierce-looking men, undoubtedly responsible for providing security to the expedition. The other two vehicles were Chinese four-wheel drive utilitarian cars suitable for transporting passengers which looked equally battered, with one driver each. One of them was led by a Mongol named Batbayar who would be the official guide of the contingent in the Gobi Desert. This man spoke Russian so that he could communicate with Aman Bodniev, and additionally spoke a little English, who knows for what reason. His temper was gentle -not very frequent in Mongolia- which contrasted with his fierce appearance. As that vehicle would lead the caravan Bodniev, Jack Berglund and Dennis would be travelling in it, so it was something like the flagship of the convoy, and the decisions about the directions to take would be made in it.

The other SUV was guided by a driver of youthful appearance and slim body whose hairless face could barely be seen under the Mongol cap. Debbie, Selma and Martín climbed into this car and settled down, sitting the former in the passenger seat and the two young people in the back seat. By the tension of the moment everyone remained silent.

Once they had made sure that all the members were aboard one of the three vehicles and that all the elements had been stored in them, the guide called Batbayar, whose window was open, took his arm out of it and with his fist hit the door giving the signal to leave; the signal was answered by the drivers of the other two vehicles confirming having received the order.

And that's how the journey began in the Gobi Desert and with it the active part of the expedition, releasing large doses of adrenaline in the members, each of whom expressed in a low voice a prayer of various religions and expressed in different languages.

Chapter 8

They had already spent a couple of hours traveling through the monotonous landscape of the desert that was becoming increasingly rugged.

Selma and Martín had fallen asleep lulled by the even rattle of the car, barely shaken by any stone in the road. Once the news that the panorama had to offer were exhausted Deborah played with her cell phone exploring certain functions that until then she had not used until she also got bored and then looked at the driver trying unsuccessfully to see his youthful features below the heavy Mongolian clothes. The woman did not even know what language the inhabitants of Mongolia speak so she could hardly expect to communicate with him. Eager to hear at least her own voice and looking at her seatmate Debbie expressed her wishes out loud.

"I would really like to ask you some questions about all this!"

Immediately after, and convinced of the uselessness of her attempt at communication, she sank into her seat in an attempt to fall asleep to shorten the travel time in the arid territory, closed her eyes and tried to disconnect herself from reality. For this reason she suffered a shock when her ears brought her the unexpected answer.

"And what would you want to ask me?"

Debbie jumped in her seat wondering if what she thought she had heard was only a figment of her imagination. In order to move with more freedom of movement in the seat she released the safety belt that had been fastened and bent so she could observe the driver's face and be able to verify a data that her ears had transmitted to her brain but to which she did not give a lot of credit.

"Do you speak English?" asked Debbie, still incredulous.

The person next to her turned and looked at her with her slanted eyes.

"That's right. What did you want to ask me?"

Upon hearing the conversation Selma and Martín woke up; the first asked her sister.

"Who were you talking to? To the driver?"

" Yes, to the driver." Before the questioning look of Selma added. "She speaks English ... and she is a young woman."

Then turned again to the driver in order to respond that she had asked.

"Well ... first of all I would like to know your name."

"Tsegseg. My name is Tsegseg."

Selma decided to participate in the conversation.

"Tsegseg. It has any meaning?"

" It means flower."

"A very romantic and aromatic name." Debbie said. "And very appropriate for a beautiful girl."

There was no answer but the woman came to perceive the blush on the girl's cheeks.

"A young woman?" Martín repeated with a somewhat vehement interest, which earned Selma a pinch. " I mean, what do you do in this desert?" The clarification was not too convincing.

Upon hearing the comment the driver of the vehicle turned her head looking at who had shown interest in her and for a moment their eyes crossed, then turned her gaze to the path in front of her.

Debbie, who had been following the whole episode in the rearview mirror, smiled when her suspicions about her sister's feelings were confirmed. Although Selma was already an adult, the protective and at the same time competitive feeling of an older sister that Debbie had always had towards her surfaced at every step.

The hours followed the hours and the miles traveled accumulated; the vastness and monotony of the desert hypnotized the travelers by immersing them in an almost permanent state of drowsiness, with eyes that rather than watching slid on the desolate panorama.

"Look, there, to our right." Martín's voice startled Debbie and Selma who were dozing. As they followed the direction the young man pointed out, they saw a scene that seemed to have been torn from an adventure novel in the Sahara desert at the end of the 19th century. On a higher hill that stood out on the horizon, the figures of a long line of what were undoubtedly camels and some others shorter, of men on horseback were cut out; a soft evening wind lifted up sand that caused the vision not to be totally clear.

"A caravan of camels! I thought it was a relic of the past." Selma's sentence had the effect of provoking the response of the driver named Tsegseg, who until then had remained silent.

"It is a reality of all times, since it is the traditional way of life and work of many of the inhabitants of the Gobi Desert."

" Are there people who inhabit these desolate places?" asked Selma, to whom the panorama produced a certain anguish.

"Yes. They live around the oases that are placed on the few springs of water. Some are sedentary and live in sets of huts or yurts. Others place their tents a little further away from the oasis but still get their supply water in it."

"Oasis!" Selma exclaimed. "It sounds romantic."

"We'll go through one of them." informed Tsegseg." The plan is to replenish water in them. I suppose that the organizers of the expedition have also planned to replenish our fuel at that site."

"The organizers?" Martín asked. " Do you know who they are?"

"I do not know them. I assumed you would know." It was the simple response of the young Mongol woman.

The line of camels was falling behind, and unexpectedly the driver added enigmatically.

"The problem of the caravans of merchants is what they attract."

"What do you mean?"

" To the bandits of the Gobi." She paused and continued. "Caravan assailants."

In the absence of new stimuli the conversation extinguished again and the passengers returned to their previous state of stupefaction. Martín noticed that Tsegseg rubbed her arms frequently and finally asked her.

"Are you tired of driving?"

" My arms fall asleep, it is due to the constant position."

"Let me replace you for a while whilst you rest."

"I shouldn't... my instructions..."

"To the devil with your instructions. My family has an old Land Rover truck with which we go everywhere, and I'm used to driving it."

Finally the girl agreed and after making a signal with the headlights to the other two vehicles stopped her car. The other drivers also stopped and waited for the change of drivers. Martín sat in the driver's seat while Tsegseg sat in the backseat next to Selma, whose eyes sparked for the kindness that the young man had had with the Mongol girl; Debbie kept following the dynamics with an amused expression.

As the Sun was hiding behind the western horizon, the first shadows began to fall on the sands and stones; Martín guided the truck concentrated in the vehicles that went ahead; Selma had fallen asleep again with her head resting on her rival's shoulder and Deborah was getting ready to enjoy her first nightfall in the bosom of the Gobi Desert. In the distance a shadow appeared on the course of the expedition.

" I wonder what in front is?" Said the driver. " It seems that we are heading towards there."

" Do you remember that I spoke about stopping in several oases? This is the first we will find."

"All right. Does it a name? Can we find it on the map?" asked Debbie while her sister woke up.

"If it really has a name, I do not know it. And I do not think it's on any map, at least on civil maps."

DEBBIE HAD PREVIOUSLY seen oasis pictures in advertising brochures promoting tours in the Gobi Desert and other sites in Mongolia, such as Lake Crescent, with its pagodas rising above the sands, its small lakes with their shores clearly cut from the sands of the desert, its yurts carefully arranged around the pond, its well-kept groves and its facilities for tourists but had always questioned the representativeness of these idyllic places as postcards of the desert. The one that opened before her and her companions on the other hand was in agreement with the preconception that the woman had of a true oasis in the arenas.

Located between two high dunes, which perhaps protected it from the strong winds of the area, the innominate oasis they approached consisted of a patch of somewhat withered vegetation around a puddle of brown water of dubious purity and contours that were lost among the sands.

The vegetation was varied and included some high species that spread a repairing shade in front of the ardor of the noon of the desert. Several miserable looking huts were scattered among the trees, corresponding to the stable sedentary population of the oasis, and a set of travelers' tents that arrived and stayed in the place for several days to replenish water were located in the surrounding sands. A background sound was noticeable in the place and caught the attention of the newcomers. As Selma made a question about it, Tsegseg pointed her finger at the heights of the neighboring dunes, where the constant winds kept the sands circulating and blurred the images of the peaks.

" The singing sands." The young Mongolian said as an explanation.

"Singing sands." Deborah repeated. " That's some poetic name."

Jack approached from the truck in which he had traveled, that was parked about fifty steps away; Dennis followed him with some gear, which he left on the floor as he ran to hug his girlfriend, after the seven hour trip without seeing her. The woman responded surprised and delighted unfolding her arms around his torso and both joined in a prolonged kiss.

"Well, it seems that the air of the desert is impregnated with romanticism." said ironically Jack.

"Envious." answered Dennis once he had finished his show of affection.

Carried by the romantic influence of the scene Selma glanced at Martín and noted with indignation that the young man did the same with the Mongolian girl.

Batbayar, the expedition guide, who had been speaking with several inhabitants of the oasis finally approached and said.

"I have obtained permission to place our camp in that grove, on the condition that we leave early tomorrow, as they wait for an important caravan to arrive.

""Have you had to pay for that permit?" asked Jack.

"Of course. Nothing is free in the desert."

The shadows had fallen on the sands, and the feverish diurnal activity of the oasis had disappeared, being replaced by groups of isolated travelers, located around numerous bonfires where the dinners of the different groups of residents and visitors were prepared.

While a couple of the Mongols prepared the food, Batbayar had displayed a large map of the Gobi in the previously flattened sands.

"We're in this place." He said pointing with his finger to an indistinguishable place in the map. "And our first destination is this other place." The finger pointed then to a spot much further south." It is approximately three hundred miles away from here."

" At this speed we will arrive tomorrow afternoon." estimated Jack.

"Right. Depending on at what time we wake up tomorrow."

" How is the road?"

"There are areas of loose sand, where the advance will be slower." The guide looked a bit worried.

"Something wrong, Batbayar?" His gesture had not gone unnoticed by Jack.

"In this area, very strong wind storms are frequent. North China is a vast sea of sand that moves easily. Many caravans have literally been covered by sand and dust and have not been seen anymore."

" Is not there a season for those storms?"

"Normally they are more frequent in March and April, in spring, but there have been very strong storms as late as the middle of November."

"I feel pretty cold." said Deborah changing abruptly the subject. "Is this also normal here?"

"The Gobi has very extreme temperature variations, from 45 ° C in the summer to 45 ° C below zero in winter, and even within a single day there are usually very strong thermal amplitudes."

After dinner the talk gradually died away and Jack finally said.

"The men have already prepared the tents and Batbayar said tomorrow we have to get up early. Let's go to sleep. There is one tent for every person, so Debbie and Selma do not need to share ."

The women withdrew and Deborah Liberman got ready to spend her first night in the desert, lulled by the singing sands.

Chapter 9

The landscape became increasingly monotonous, the desert of stones and sand turned into a soil covered by fine particles of silica that the vehicles raised in their ride; the passengers had to hermetically close the windows to restrict the entrance of the annoying dust to the cabins, but without being able to completely prevent it from entering. The interior air of the vans gradually became unbreathable, forcing travelers to cover their noses and mouths with scarves and kerchiefs, and their eyes with goggles to avoid eye irritation. They had already traveled three hours at reduced speed to avoid increasing the problem but it became evident that as they approached the Chinese border they were entering more and more into an ocean of sand.

Jack, who was sitting in the passenger seat in the front row of the vehicle in front noticed that the usually talkative guide was muted and clutching the steering wheel of the vehicle with total concentration, so he decided not to interfere with the driving making any questions.

The cars had broken the formation of Indian line that they had kept up to that moment and advanced in parallel forming a front to avoid being wrapped in the curtain of sand that each one raised in his ride.

At one point Batbayar, still without breaking his silence, pointed with his index finger to a thin dark segment that could be seen on the southern horizon. The sky above that line had turned dark and the whole sky and earth were taking a sinister look as the seconds passed.

Finally Dennis, who was sitting in the back row decided to break the silence and addressing the guide asked.

"Batbayar. What is happening? What is it that we are heading to?" The guide responded nervously.

"We are not heading towards it but it's coming towards us."

"What is it?" Asked uneasily Jack.

"It's ... a dust storm."

THE AMERICAN HAD ALREADY heard of the terrible storms of fine sand that rise in the Gobi Desert and go towards Chinese territory but also to the north, covering not only caravans and travelers but towns, cities and crops, ruining the respiratory health of the population, spoiling their crops, killing livestock and burying innumerable travelers who were on their way.

"Can we change course?" Dennis insisted.

"There is no way to escape, the storm is coming on us." Batbayar answered." We can only stay on course and try to cross it through."

"And pray." added Jack.

Indeed, what had once been a simple stripe on the horizon already acquired relief and thickness and was clearly distinguished as a cloud of light brown color with darker veins. The first particles of sand, ahead of the storm, began to whip the windscreen of the vehicles and the atmosphere before them was becoming less clear. The travelers had their eyes fixed on the ominous spot that grew by leaps and bounds. In the vehicle that transported them Selma, in panic, clung to the arms of Martín who tried to shelter her and cover her head to avoid the threatening spectacle. Debbie, in the passenger seat, looked straight ahead at the cloud, watching it gain height as it closed in on the dark sky. In a couple of minutes the giant brown cloud was on them and swallowed the vehicles that stopped seeing each other. The passengers lost sight of the stretch of desert that extended in front of them and in a matter of seconds they did not see the hood of the engine of the car in which they were traveling; the visibility was reduced to zero while what had been a strong whistle of the wind was transformed into a deafening roar. Shaken by the blizzard the vehicles were shaking to both sides threatening to overturn.

Finally the monstrous cloud covered completely the whole landscape, the engines stopped working due to the contamination that covered the carburetors and injection pumps. A gust of wind took the truck sideways, made it skid, lifted it into its sinister bosom and spun it around. Nature piously disconnected the brains of the crew of the vehicles while outside the elements unleashed furiously in the middle of the gloomy roar of the wind.

Deborah felt someone was vigorously shaking her right arm. She partially opened her eyes, which fortunately had been protected from the dust by her goggles, but when the woman tried to breathe her airways were clogged and she involuntarily coughed to clear them. Also her mouth was full of sand and she had to spit to be able to talk. Only then did she realize that the driver Tsegseg was the one who had awakened her from her fading. Debbie smiled weakly; she had already noticed the Mongol's courage and integrity when she watched her drive through the storm's hubbub, before they both lost consciousness. A feeling of admiration for the girl had grown inside her.

"Come on, help me with the other two." Said the young woman.

At that time Deborah took charge of the situation around her. The van in which they were traveling, after several turns on itself pushed by the wind, had been left resting on its four wheels although the interior was a chaos of packages and equipment. She looked out with fear because of the recent memory and was surprised to see a clear sky after the storm. Looking around, the woman saw that Jack, Dennis and Batbayar were pushing their vehicle to turn it over since it was overturned. Of the other truck there was no news.

Deborah unbuckled her seatbelt and with difficulty opened the door on her side because of the accumulated sand in front of it. She entered the back of the truck and helped Tsegseg to succor Selma and Martín. The woman sighed with relief when she saw that both of them were breathing and moving, although Martín was dripping blood from an injury in his forehead probably caused by some heavy object in the overturning.

"Wait! I need to find the emergency kit in all this marasmus ." said Debbie. " Luckily you do not need stitches."

At that moment Dennis approached and immediately hugged his girlfriend; then he extended his hand to his relative, telling him.

" You wanted to come to the East for adventures? Well, you cannot complain."

Martín was going to respond but he could only emit a cry of pain caused by the fact that Debbie was placing disinfectant in the bleeding wound. Tsegseg was reviving Selma, checking that all she had was a panic attack but no external wounds.

Jack also went to check the status of his companions.

"These two vehicles and the people that were traveling in them are relatively well. We will have some work to restart the engines. But we could not find the truck with the four custodians. It is not in sight, it simply disappeared from the landscape."

Slowly the expedition members succeeded in restoring order in both vehicles. Jack and Batbayar concentrated on trying to clean the car's injection and ignition circuits while the Mongolian, Debbie, Dennis and Martín began walk around looking for a mound of sand that could be covering the missing truck. Selma fell prey to terror inside her vehicle, refusing to leave it.

The four had already moved in all directions in their search when they finally heard the voice of Tsegseg, coming from a distant location more than three hundred meters away.

"Here! Here they are." She shouted pointing to a dune more than twenty meters high, which she had been digging with her hands until a window was visible.

Everyone ran to join her, aware that it was imperative to uncover the vehicle by removing the sand blanket to allow the air to reach the inside of it.

Finally they were able to free one of the doors and allow two of the occupants to stagger out of the truck, sitting on the floor and trying to catch their breath. When continuing with the excavation they removed the other bodies of the interior, verifying that unfortunately one of them was without life, evidently suffocated by the sand that covered him.

At that moment they heard a couple of explosions that told them that Batbayar had managed to start his truck. Dennis greeted with his arm and his gesture was answered by the Mongol who was on his way to the other van to repeat the procedure.

By nightfall they had managed to recover the three vehicles, most of the cargo fortunately including water and fuel. It was time to take charge of the dead custodian, for whom they dug a grave in the sand to prevent the vermin from devouring his body. The Mongols lit a bonfire and sat in a circle around the place where their companion rested. One of the men extracted a curious string instrument with which he began to perform a monotonous and plaintive melody while his companions accompanied with a strange song consisting of guttural sounds that repeated what appeared to be a mantra.

While this was happening the other travelers formed a silent circle keeping a respectful silence for the comrade who would remain in those desolate expanses of the Gobi Desert.

Chapter 10

The departure from the place where the storm had surprised them was sad and the dejection was evident in all the faces, particularly those of the Mongol custodians, whom the desert had snatched from a companion and perhaps a relative. Before leaving the place Jack approached the men to fraternize with them, even though there was no common language in which they could make themselves understood. From a distance Bodniev watched him approvingly, while the others stared in a respectful silence.

In the expedition there had been a moral break as the members verified, especially the most novice in real adventures, the fragility of existence in the middle of the vast desert with its harsh rules, some of them unknown and unpredictable, since from the sighting of the storm on the horizon until its unleashing above their heads had not elapsed more than half an hour.

The change that had taken place on the surface of the desert was evident. The mixture of landscapes of areas covered with stones with sand and some patches of hard grass had given place to another panorama where only the siliceous dust of a monotonous beige color existed and the horizon was covered by the high dunes whose location varied with every gale. In some sections the travelers could see skeletons of camels and horses that had been covered by some wind and uncovered by other winds that had come later. Debbie wondered the remains of how many caravans would lie beneath those ubiquitous dunes.

After traveling all morning they made a stop next to one of the few rocky outcroppings that at least gave them a bit of shade and relief from the heat of the air at that time, after having spent a cold night. As it was said before, the Gobi's thermal amplitude is one of the largest in the world and this forced them to change their clothes several times a day to feel comfortable.

The shaman had climbed nimbly to the top of the rock, which rose about thirty meters above the level of the surrounding desert. Screening with one hand over his eyes to avoid the glare produced by the reflection of the sun's rays on the sand, he looked insistently in a fixed direction and his gesture looked worried. Jack and Dennis decided to climb also in order to look at the expanding horizon from that height.

"What are you looking at, Aman?" asked Jack.

Without answering the Siberian pointed his finger in the direction he was looking at. At first the two Americans did not distinguish anything, but after a while of adapting their eyes to the prevailing luminosity Dennis exclaimed.

"There is a slight glow that appears and disappears. It looks metallic."

Bodniev shook his head in a negative gesture.

"It is the reflection of sunlight on binoculars." His voice denoted concern. "They are sweeping the horizon and that is why at certain moments the shine disappears."

"Who do you think they can be? Members of a caravan?" asked Dennis.

"We must assume the most negative hypothesis. Something like a worst case scenario." answered the Siberian. "And be ready for it."

" And what would that hypothesis be?"

Without answering immediately the Russian began to descend from the top of the rock. In a moment he snapped.

"Highwaymen. Mongolian bandits."

Dennis looked at Jack questioningly; the runologist said.

"I know their reputation by hearsay. They are ruthless assailants of caravans. They steal everything including horses and camels, and leave the victims whom they have not killed abandoned in the desert to die dehydrated in the sands."

" Do you think they have seen us too?"

"I do not know, but as Bodniev said we must assume that they have done it and prepare us for that case. Come, let's go down!"

Upon descending they saw with some intrigue that the Siberian had first come close and talked reservedly to Tsegseg, who listened attentively, they then approached Batbayar and the rest of the guards. Dennis, who did not miss any detail of the Russian's actions asked his companion.

" Have you seen the order in which Bodniev proceeded? First he talked with Tsegseg and then with the guards. I wonder what it means."

" I cannot explain it either."

All the expedition members met together summoned by the Russian, who proceeded to narrate his sighting but without giving explanations. Then Dennis, who had had military training for a couple of years after leaving university, proceeded to instruct on the measures to be taken.

"The shadows will begin to fall within a couple of hours. We cannot risk entering the desert if we have doubts that there are potentially hostile people in front of us."

"Can´t we go backwards, get away from this place, retrace our steps?" asked Debbie obviously frightened.

"Go backwards? Where? We have the same desert behind us that we have in front of us. No! I believe that these rocks in which we are now located give us the best spot to prepare a defense, if this proves to be necessary. This cliff will cover our backs and from it we will have a privileged firing range."

Dennis was silent and looked at the other members of the expedition. Bodniev and Jack nodded and the former addressed the Mongol custodians to explain the situation and the decision made. Apparently there was consensus regarding the measures to be applied and the defense tactics began to be put into practice. The three vehicles were arranged in a semicircle in front of the rock, and they tried to mask them with sand with not much success, while also covering the spaces under the chassis with sand. Two of the Mongol warriors armed with their rifles climbed to the top of the rock, from which they could cover a wide and deep observation field. Deborah and Selma were located in a crack in the rock, which had a certain depth but did not form a cave. There they dedicated themselves to prepare the food while there was some light, because they could not light fires that would give away their position in the middle of the night.

Bodniev, Jack, Dennis, Martín, Batbayar and the other two Mongols stood at the different points of the semicircle of vehicles and Martín saw with astonishment that suddenly long weapons appeared for all, of which they had no previous news. Dennis walked a hundred paces forward to judge the defense device, and after a careful examination said sarcastically when he returned.

"It is the modern version of the circle of carts to defend against the Indians in the Wild West."

Selma approached the place where Martín was. Her gesture showed uneasiness. Following an impulse the young man put an arm around her shoulders and brought her close to him. The girl breathed a sigh but showed a relief to feel the male hug. Suddenly she asked.

"And Tsegseg? Do you know where she is?"

" I have not seen her for a while. I had not noticed her absence."

Shadows covered the rock and the surrounding sands and a long vigil began in the desert.

Deborah slept soundly after an exhausting day. In her agitated dreams she heard a distant and dull rumble, like an advancing litany, turned from one side to the other and the noise ceased; then a moment of silence that although psychologically prolonged lasted only for a few moments and finally a neighing. It was this last sound that woke her startled. She sat on the sand floor not understanding what had happened and continued to pay attention without perceiving anything else. Already awake, she bent over to the place where she knew Dennis was, guiding herself through the shadows and feeling the way. When she reached the man's side, Debbie noticed that he was talking in whispers with another person who turned out to be Bodniev. Apparently the young man had asked a question and the Siberian answered.

"They have covered the hooves of their horses with rags to muffle the sounds. Now they have dismounted and are probably approaching in the middle of the shadows." Then he made a silence after which he murmured.

"They will attack with the sunrise, with the first light of dawn."

Chapter 11

Fifteen shadows crawled across the sandy floor in the total darkness that preceded the dawn. They carried their weapons and other metallic objects on top of them to prevent them from rubbing against stones on the ground and producing noises that could alert the besieged enemies of their presence.

The advance was necessarily slow but they were not in a hurry because they could not attack in the depths of the night at the risk of hurting their own companions with friendly fire. The men communicated with each other by very slight whistles that barely traveled about 3 or 4 meters before becoming extinct. They were advancing on a wide front that completely surrounded the cliff and their progress was coordinated so that everyone was at the same distance of all others at each moment. They kept crawling in the greatest silence in an attack that had undoubtedly been successfully carried out on other occasions.

Shortly after two of the shadows passed sliding on each side of a small mound that barely protruded from the flat ground it suddenly moved slightly and a small shadow began to stand silently up shaking the sand that had covered it until then. In complete secrecy, it bent close to the two shadows that had surpassed it immediately before. Due to the lack of light of the new moon no metallic flash reflected the sharp blade in its upward movement to take impulse and then down, only the hiss of the wind produced by the saber moving downwards betrayed what happened. The blade fell with precision despite the lack of light and cut off the head of the man who was crawling on the ground to the right. The Mongol on the left had a hunch of what was happening and turned his head to the danger that was coming. An agonized cry cut the deep silence of the desert produced by the man's last breath before his head was also cut off by the sharp blade of Mongolian steel.

After the scream the entire desert area was disturbed like a beaten hive. Some of the shadows that approached the rock rose and began to run towards it while others turned against the danger that had arisen behind them and the squeaking of the clash of swords covered the howls of the attackers.

Suddenly some rays of light coming from the spotlights installed on the roofs of the trucks illuminated the scene and a half dozen shots resounded loudly and their echo bounced in the hitherto silent desert. At that moment the first rays of sunlight appeared on the eastern horizon and spread throughout the scene

Martín fired with many doubts and saw how the man on whom he had aimed collapsed, joining the bundles that lay on the ground. At one point the leader of the attackers, seeing his strategy derailed, took a horn out of his clothes and touched retreat, so that the survivors fled, leaving seven bodies in the field. Minutes later, the attenuated sound of the hooves of horses moving away at full speed was the sequel to the disastrous end of the attack.

Bodniev, Batbayar, Jack, Dennis and Martín emerged from behind the semicircle of trucks carrying their weapons and approached the battlefield. The two Americans followed the trail of the fugitives to make sure they had effectively fled. The Russian and Batbayar inspected the fallen and a couple of shots informed that two wounded writhing on the ground had been finished off in that primitive fight in the desolate desert.

With a gesture of ecstasy on his face Martín advanced towards the figure that stood on the stage of the fight still holding a saber covered in blood in her hand. The young man had already recognized Tsegseg in that character, but the Mongol woman was transfigured.

Instead of the modest girl dressed in a Mao style brown coat and trousers, now Martín was standing in front of a warrior with wide, multi-colored wide pants tightened at the ankles and a short red cloth vest that barely allowed it to cover the small breasts. Her own sweat and other people's blood covered her body. At the sight of the approaching boy Tsegseg dropped the saber to the ground. With a rapt gesture Martín opened his arms and wrapped them around her. Looking from afar Selma inclined her head, seeing her secretly guarded illusions fall to pieces.

The travelers spent several hours digging tombs at the foot of the rock in which they deposited the bodies of the seven fallen bandits. The rest of the afternoon passed with other tasks of preparation for the next stage, so that only at five p.m. they were in condition to leave. As there was very little light left Jack decided to stay that night under the protection of the rock, which had given them such good services until that moment. One of the Mongols who officiated as cook and Deborah prepared an early dinner and set a fire, this time without fear.

"It will even keep away the animals that are hanging around alerted by the smell of blood." explained Aman Bodniev.

"What kind of animals are there in this desert?" asked startled Selma.

"Very likely some types of feline exist in these solitudes, and they will be short of food in this season."

"Where are Tsegseg and Martín? " Asked casually Jack. Dennis gestured for silence and then approached him and whispered.

"We have not seen them since the end of the fight. My relative was transfixed by the vision of the warrior woman. He had already shown obvious signs of falling in love with her before."

"It's a girl who radiates magnetism and power."

"And an aura of mystery around her." added Deborah as she joined the two men without being noticed by them.

"I am interested in hearing a feminine opinion about Tsegseg." Dennis said in an objective tone, and then added . "Debbie is very insightful in matters of interpersonal relationships."

"The girl had already marked Martín from the first moment we got into the truck driven by her, and with subtle gestures has been weaving a loop around him. The boy was seduced by her from the beginning."

"I had not noticed that. I thought Martín was interested in your sister."

" He is a good-looking young man and a little candid, very prone to fall under the influence of a woman of strong temperament."

"How is your sister with these news?"

"Devastated. It seems to me that she had made illusions of which she was not even aware."

At that moment Batbayar joined the group and announced that dinner was ready.

The Mongols had made a separate group and the guide was approaching his countrymen when Bodniev asked him to join the travelers.

"We are going to make a summary of what happened on this day." said the Russian. "Let's start with the military part, which I leave up to you." He added referring to Dennis.

"Although we had not that explicit purpose on mind, the defense device we had armed worked like an ambush, or rather, a counter-ambush. The surprise element that the bandits tried to use did not work because you, Aman, warned us that they were coming for us."

"It's true." added Jack, addressing the Russian. "How did you know?"

" It was an ... intuition. I already told you that they are like flashes that go through my mind."

"But the armed defense would not have been of help without the unexpected participation of Tsegseg." continued Dennis.

"What did the girl actually do?" asked Debbie.

"My conclusion is that she lay in the desert about a hundred meters in front of this rock." continued Dennis pointing to the cliff. "... and covered herself with sand with the sword in her hand. There she must have waited patiently for the bandits to pass crawling by her side on their way to the rock and then she fell from the rear with her fearsome weapon, which killed two of them, and especially put us on guard of what was happening."

"How did she know in what way they were going to attack us? " Asked Jack." How did she foresee that they were going to approach during the night crawling on the floor?"

"That is a usual technique in the Mongol hordes." Batbayar joined the conversation for the first time."They advance crouched to fall on their victims with the first light of dawn. Tsegseg knows those tactics."

"Which brings us to the real question." added Aman addressing Batbayar." Who is really Tsegseg?"

Chapter 12

Batbayar shifted uncomfortably on the floor where he was sitting.
"You must tell us everything." Urged Jack. "You, your men and our group are risking our lives together in this adventure."

Batbayar reflected for a moment and then his face showed that he had made a decision.

"Tsegseg is the firstborn daughter and heiress of the head of our horde."

"Who is the boss of that horde?" inquired Bodniev.

"Ata Khan." replied succinctly Batbayar. The Russian let out an exhalation, then added.

"All right. Go on."

"Tsegseg is a beautiful young woman but has been raised by Buddhist monks as a warrior. Her father has prepared her to assume the direction of the horde, since he plans to retire soon to a monastery."

" How did you both join our group? " Asked Jack. "Who recruited you?"

"The decision was made by Ata Khan himself. He ordered my men and I to join this contingent and appointed Tsegseg as our leader." The Mongol took a moment before proceeding. "You must not fear, our orders are to protect you from the dangers of the Gobi."

"But I do not think that Ata Khan has become the protector of all the foreigners that wander in the desert." Reasoned Bodniev. "Why us? What makes us special?"

"The truth is that I do not know. Maybe Tsegseg has the answer. I am just a soldier of the horde, as are my men." Batbayar stood up and added." Now I must go with them.

"Of course." Jack concluded. "Go with your people."

"But first tell me something." Added Debbie "What is Tsegseg looking for in Martín?"

Batbayar looked surprised with the question.

"Most probably what every woman looks for in a man. Let me tell you something. When a young Mongolian woman wants to get a man, she does not stop until she gets him."

The moment Batbayar left, Selma appeared and silently joined the group formed by her sister, Jack, Dennis and Bodniev. The girl's face had evidence of having cried but now she looked calm.

"What we heard today from Batbayar alters everything we had assumed regarding our expedition." stated Jack in a serious voice.

"What do you mean?" asked Debbie with a gesture of surprise.

"We thought that our Bluthund group was in charge of all this search, but we see that another powerful group has joined us with its own agenda, with intentions that we really do not know." Jack made a moment of silence and then asked.

" Tell me, Aman. When Batbayar mentioned that Ata Khan you exhaled a sigh. What do you know about him?"

"It is a legendary figure in Outer Mongolia and throughout Central Asia. He is the current link in an ancient dynasty of Mongol leaders that allegedly dates back to Genghis Khan, of whom Ata is said to be a descendant. His horde is composed of five or six thousand Mongolian warriors whom, although they live scattered in the deserts, he can summon in a short time by mysterious means. I have even heard that his personal project is to restore the monarchy in what is the current Republic of Mongolia starting with the remains of the Golden Horde."

"A utopian initiative." Answered Dennis.

"Never underestimate the push of the Mongols. The Russians have been trying to stop them for centuries."

"What is Ata Khan's relationship with Bluthund?" inquired Dennis.

"The truth is that I do not know. My contacts simply told me that this Batbayar would be waiting for us with an escort group and that we can rely on them."

Tsegseg was smiling. With one hand she caressed the head that the young man had placed in her lap while the events of the day paraded in her mind. She looked at Martín and confirmed that he was sleeping. They had lain on a small patch of withered herbs under the shelter of small rocks and had sex until they were exhausted.

Tsegseg had had a victorious day. The Buddhist lama who had instructed her in martial arts and war tactics would be proud of her disciple's performance in the battle with the Gobi bandits, desert rats that her father wanted to eliminate as a prerequisite of his plans. Also the main concubine of his father would be satisfied with the way in which her student had put into practice her lessons of love arts overflowing with eroticism.

In a moment Martín moved his head on her belly and Tsegseg decided to wake him up.

"Get dressed, you must go get my work clothes from the truck, which I left under the driver's seat."

"I like you more in this odalisque costume."

"Not of odalisque, silly, but of warrior. But now it is full of dried blood. I will have to wash them in the first oasis we find."

Martín returned after a while with the requested clothes. The girl took off the costume she was wearing, leaving naked her splendid female body, while Martín watched her delighted. In a moment he took one of her little feet between his hands and kissed it.

"Stop. We must return to the camp."

Ignoring her command the young man stretched out on the grass next to her.

"Tell me, Tsegseg, why me?"

"What do you mean?"

"It is clear that you have chosen me for some reason. Why me, even though I am not a warrior?"

"Simply because I like you. That is the plain reason why we Mongol women choose our men. As I told you before, I am the daughter of a powerful leader and I have inherited from him the decision to go and get what I want."

" What is your father's daughter doing, acting as a driver in a risky expedition?"

The girl took a few moments to meditate if she should communicate her secret; finally reflected that since she had conquered the man she wanted she should now trust him; in any case, she had him under her yoke, a sweet but iron yoke.

" Waiting for the opportunity to return to my people what belongs to them."

"What do you mean? What is it about?"

"You will know in due course."

The two youngsters returned to the camp when the others had finished eating. No one made any comments or asked any questions. Only Debbie approached them and said.

"We've put your dinner apart. Sit there, I'm going to warm it up again."

Martín noticed Selma's fleeting look and immediately knew what to attribute it to. Paradoxically Deborah gave him a smile the moment their eyes met.

That night, when Dennis and Martín were in the tent they shared the first one, who had been struggling with the question of whether or not to talk about the issue he had in mind with his relative, finally said.

"Martín, I think you should know that Tsegseg is a daughter ..."

" Of a warrior leader named Ata Khan, I know. I also know about his projects for the Mongolian nation."

Dennis could not help but wonder if the young man had become a cog in those projects. To what extent could loving infatuation and sexual impulses change a young person's cultural veneer? But the real question was, to what extent could Bluthund continue to trust him as they had until then?

Thus, the first conflict with external agents to which the expedition was confronted generated a series of questions and rethinking within it.

Chapter 13

The secretary observed her image in the mirror placed in the entrance hall. She sharpened her critical sense but everything seemed in order; her blonde hair was neither too short nor too long and was pulled back in a tight way, actually a bit old fashioned but suitable for the organization for which she worked; the light blue blouse on a tight bodice, the skirt barely covering the knee so to insinuate but not show her splendid legs.

<*Alles in Ordnung*> she finally decided. Only then did she approach the majestic massive wooden door that led to the chief's office. According to the drill, she gave two blows with her knuckles, neither too strong nor too light, and without waiting for instructions from inside opened the door, surprised once again by checking how light it was for such a heavy structure. Once inside she waited for the old man sitting in the vast desk on a two-step platform that placed him above the level of possible assistants to pay attention. The man removed his glasses, exposing his big blue eyes.

THE GOBI CODEX - LOST TREASURE BEYON A FLEEING HORIZON

"*Ja, bitte, Frau Schmiddel*, I listen to you."

Only once the boss had addressed her, Gerda Schmiddel replied.

"*Herr Direktor*, Hans Wildau has entered the building. He is coming directly to this floor."

"Well, please show him in it as soon as he arrives."

A few minutes later the routine was repeated; the secretary knocked on the door, opened it and let in a handsome man of about forty-five, athletic build and blond hair also combed back in an old fashion.

"*Herr Direktor*." He said staying at the door and tilting his head slightly.

"Do you need anything else?" Asked the secretary.

" Yes, Gerda. Please bring us two coffees."

The director stood up, went forward to the newcomer, extending his hand.

"Nice to see you Hans, please sit down with me." He said pointing to a small table in a corner of the immense office, actually a show room.

The secretary came back with the coffees and the Director told her.

"Thanks Gerda. That will be everything for now."

Then he turned to Wildau who was still waiting to be addressed by his superior.

"Well Hans, you gave us a scare in Kazakhstan. We were for a while without news from you..."

"Exactly twenty-three days Herr *Direktor*."

" All that time you were kidnapped?"

"*Ja! Herr Direktor*."

In reality, the superior envied Wildau who, because of his responsibilities and age, could still live adventures that had been banned to him since he got trapped by bureaucratic issues twenty years before.

"I want to hear all the details."

THE GOBI CODEX- LOST TREASURE BEYON A FLEEING HORIZON

THE MAN CALLED WILDAU knew the director's avidity for the details of extreme experiences, and his true interest in his subordinates, so he had prepared a written narration of the whole episode, which he related by adding further details and answering the boss's questions. Once finished the director said.

"Bravo Hans, I can imagine the anguish you've been through. Would you mind leaving with me that kind of report you wrote? You know that I like to have narrations of everything that our people have done."

"Of course Herr Direktor." said Wildau handing the paper over.

"Now, tell me about the new topic. I understand that Bluthund and in particular our friend Jack Berglund are back in action."

"That's right."

"Good man this Jack Berglund."

"Indeed, he is."

"But he is not one of us."

"No, that's clear."

"And how were our relations with him?"

"In the end relatively well. There is no doubt that at the beginning we harmed him but finally you managed to get him out of jail." (*)

* cf. Runes of Blood, by the same author

"Well, tell me what they're doing now, I mean Bluthund and Jack Berglund."

"For what we know they are looking for a treasure in the Gobi Desert, on the border between Mongolia and China."

" A treasure there? What treasure?"

"You may remember Baron Ungern von Sternberg."

" Yes, he was one of the enemies of the Bolsheviks during the war that followed the Communist Revolution of 1917. A very brave but eccentric character."

" Who supported the conspiracy of a local king who for a time evicted the hierarchs of the Republic of Mongolia from power."

" I believe that von Ungern was finally shot by the Bolsheviks."

"That's how he ended. But first he consigned his best men to the task of taking away the treasure of the Mongol royal family."

"Ah! Yes, yes. I remember something about it, but I always thought it was a legend."

"It is what the successors of von Ungern divulged, to avoid attracting treasure hunters. Only that it might not be a legend."

"Well, but it is not related to what interests us. That happened in Mongolia and not in Tibet, and I do not understand what could be the reason for our eventual involvement. We are not treasure hunters. Or is there a relationship after all?"

Wildau tilted her body slightly forward as if to communicate something confidential.

"Listen to this, Mr. Director ..."

After a private conversation of more than an hour Wildau got up from his chair, greeted very politely the Director and left the office. As he passed by Frau Schmiddel's desk, he shook her hand in a very formal way, even though he winked. Then he walked out to the lift lobby, where no sign announced whose office it was or what was its business.

Gerda Schmiddel unrolled a small piece of paper that Wildau had left in her hand and found that the name of a discreet hotel, a room number, and the number of a cell phone were written on it.

Despite being married to a much older man, Gerda maintained a discreet relationship with Wildau, which materialized every time the man was in New York. The truth was that she was madly in love with him.

The Director rose from his chair and climbed down from the platform on which his desk was installed. He walked to the large window and drew the curtains. Since the office was on a 19th floor, he had an ample view of Broadway, which at that time was an anthill of people. The day was bright and the man closed his eyes. The memories of his childhood in the misty Black Forest came to his mind; in two months time he would make his annual pilgrimage to his birthplace which would also include going to meet his superiors. He hoped this time he would be able to bring them conclusive clues of what he had been revealing from previous decades, and he trusted Wildau to achieve those clues. What his subordinate had just entrusted to him lit a new light on a vital subject that had remained in the shadows after the fall of the Third Reich. Neither the Director nor his organization were Nazis, and they never had been, but all of them had with Nazis a certain common interpretation of History and Nature.

The news was that the flamboyant Baron von Ungern had shared some beliefs that ten or fifteen years later a nucleus of occultists would offer the rising Fuhrer. Not only did he share them, but in his time of rule in Mongolia the Baron had carried out his own apparently promising investigations and registered them, although it was not known in what form.

Would it be possible that this time ...? The Director shook his head. He did not want to entertain excessive expectations, but the truth was that that achievement was a central objective of his life.

Arriving at his hotel Hans Wildau showered, dressed in a robe and after consulting the clock took his cell phone and dialed a number that had saved in the memory as "Bluthund". At the third pulse someone attended the other side.

"I'm Hans." He identified himself.

The other greeted him in a similarly short manner.

" Do you have news of Berglund and his people?"

" No, since they left Chojr we have lost track of them. It is evident that they are somewhere in the Gobi Desert."

" Did you call Berglund's girlfriend, that Indian woman ... What's her name?"

"Dhawan, Lakshmi Dhawan."

"...did you call her to find out if she has news?"

"Yes, I talked to her five days ago, and she had not received any calls. I do not want to call her again. She works with the FBI, is very insightful and I do not want her to become suspicious."

"Well, let me know if you have any news."

"All right. You do the same."

Both men ended the call in unison, since they knew that short calls were less likely to be tracked.

Wildau lay back on the bed and fell asleep from exhaustion. He woke up suddenly, looked at the clock and jumped off the bed. He did not want to be late for the meeting with Gerda. He planned that both would get drunk that night because he knew the level of disinhibition to which the woman arrived in that state. Then Wildau would practice with her certain love arts that he had learned in the East in the arms of certain exotic women. But her interest in Gerda was not merely sexual, he had known for a long time that the woman was in love with him even though he could not pin down his own feelings. Due to the Germanic stubbornness of both those feelings had not come to light but this time Hans Wildau was willing to clarify the issue in the middle of the ecstasy of passion.

Chapter 14

D ennis had verified the coordinates he had obtained with the GPS by means of the usual astronomical procedure not so much because he distrusted the former but because he felt sympathy for the use of the sextant.

"We are practically on the border with China." He said in a low voice.

THE GOBI CODEX- LOST TREASURE BEYON A FLEEING HORIZON

"There is no sign in view of the limit." commented Debbie in a gesture of surprise.

"What did you expect in the midst of these solitudes? A welcome sign in several languages?"

"Don't be rude."

Regretfully the man came over and kissed her on the forehead. At that moment Bodniev appeared behind them; obviously the Siberian had heard Dennis's comment.

"I'm going out for a while, while you prepare dinner."

"It's getting dark, do not take too long." Warned the worried woman.

" Leave him, he knows how to take care of himself. Besides, I have the feeling that what he has to do must be done alone."

"What do you mean?"

"Don't forget that he is basically a clairvoyant, and that he is expected to guide us in our search. I suppose he's going to look for some solitary place to meditate."

Indeed Bodniev walked for a long time until he reached a place that internally inspired him confidence; he then moved several rocks to use them as a seat and gathered the few dry woods and bunches of herbs that some distant rainy season had left in that area of the desert. He lit a fire and sat on the stones to wait. Something from within would indicate when it would be time to act. He began to swing very gently in his stony seat while a whisper came out of his mouth, in the form of a strange melody with repetitive phrases that evidently corresponded to a mantra. He took his large backpack and from it extracted a small flat drum that he began to strike with one hand, while staring at the flames. At one point he reached into the backpack again and extracted this time a handful of dried herbs, selected and collected in his native Siberia. Then he threw them into the fire where they began to crackle and produce an acrid smoke. The shaman put his face close to the fire in order to fully inhale the smoke and began to hammer more violently the drum as he raised the tone of his voice. The Russian remained in that form for a prolonged period until he suddenly became silent and remained quiet. Then he got up and uttered certain words of some forgotten Siberian language that even he could not understand. He was exhausted from the effort of concentration he had made but satisfied with the result of the initiatory journey. He threw sand on the fire to fully extinguish it and kept his ritual elements; then he began a slow return to the camp.

The travelers gathered around a campfire where they were dining and watched him pass in silence and enter his tent, which unlike the others was not an industrial camping product but it had been made by the same Bodniev with animal skins and was quite heavy.

Jack followed him with his eyes and commented in a low voice.

"I think tomorrow we will have news."

When Debbie opened the tent door Selma woke up surprised to see her sister already fully dressed.

"What time is it?"

"Time to leave. Get up, sleepy! The men have already stored everything in the vehicles and only this tent is left to be kept."

As usual, the truck driven by Batbayar went to the front. Bodniev gave indications every so often to the driver on the direction to take, while Dennis with a compass in his hand marked on the map the course taken by the expedition. After about an hour of travel the landscape began to change becoming more undulated, with rocky outcrops becoming more frequent and higher. Finally, elevations appeared on the horizon though they did not constitute a mountain range. The Russian sharpened his eyesight so that his eyes became two lines until he suddenly abandoned his almost total silence with a gesture of unexpected excitement.

"There they are ... the camel's humps."

"What the hell are you talking about. There aren´t any camels around?" Dennis asked bewildered, while Jack smiled, pointing to two hills that rose to the east and that somehow resembled the back of a camel.

" Is that what you have seen in your visions?" asked Dennis what was answered by an affirmative gesture by the Russian.

" They are just as I saw them in my vision in Siberia." He added exultantly.

While the caravan was approaching the elevations Bodniev indicated to set course for the depression of the earth between both humps of the allegorical camel.

" Will there be a practicable path in that area?"" Batbayar asked.

"Yes." was the laconic response of the Russian.

They headed toward the depression between the high hills and soon Dennis pointed to a narrow passage between the rocks. Bodniev nodded and the caravan entered the gorge without really knowing if it would lead somewhere or if they could retrace their steps if not; it was the first of many crucial decisions that they should take along the way.

The vehicles shuddered strongly when passing over large boulders that the drivers could not always avoid and at times it was difficult for them to advance against certain obstacles that even the traction in the four wheels could not overcome. Several times all the occupants had to descend to push the trucks in order to unclog them. After reaching a high point the trail began to descend and widened, giving a respite to the engines and drivers.

Dennis was filming the scene on both sides and recording a description with the camera microphone of what he saw in front.

" We are descending towards a valley contoured by hills in all its periphery. Forward the arid panorama of the Gobi seems to be transformed into a more friendly landscape, with herbs covering the descending slopes of the mountains. It is likely that the circle of low hills create a microclimate that retains some moisture. I wonder if the orography will raise the winds of the desert so that they pass over and do not dehydrate this valley."

Meanwhile they had reached a depression surrounded by higher bushes and Dennis gave an order to Batbayar.

" Stop here. I want to see what's there in the middle of those pastures."

He got out of the vehicle and walked about two hundred steps until he reached the designated place. He bowed and when he got up he started making gestures urging the others to come closer.

"It is a well with water." He exclaimed enthusiastically. "Bring canteens and drums to replace what we have consumed. We will purify it later."

When arriving at the place Deborah verified that indeed a well existed of approximately circular form had a diameter of about thirty meters with a surface of about one hundred square meters. The edges were muddy but the liquid towards the center of the pond looked cleaner. Dennis took off his boots and rolled up his trousers and, taking two of the twenty liter drums, walked into the water, followed by three of the Mongols who exhibited similar enthusiasm for the unexpected gift of nature.

" All right. We will establish a camp here. We are very tired, we need to bathe and warm a decent meal." said Jack, who was the one who normally made the decisions of the trip. "Now we are going to refill with water the radiators of the trucks, although we will previously filter it."

As is often the case in the desert, water changed for the better everybody´s mood. The night came over in that festive and relaxed atmosphere and while the women and the Mongolian cook prepared the dinner the men washed the vehicles removing the thick layer of desert dust that was inside and on top of them.

After eating the groups gathered around two cheerful fires that propitiated the conversation.

"Is this the place you have visualized in your trances?" Dennis asked addressing the Siberian.

" Without a doubt, it is inside this enclosure that the men of von Ungern deposited their treasure, whatever it was that it contained."

"But ... Do you have more details of where it can be? This valley has an area of many hectares."

"I have seen the men excavating and I think that once we are in it, I will be able to individualize it, but we must find it first."

"How do you plan to do it?" insisted Debbie.

"Every day has its tasks. Tomorrow we will search." While saying this Bodniev directed a suggestive look at Selma that only Deborah captured, but refrained from asking questions.

Indeed the next day, after the frugal breakfast and while the Mongols were doing their work to establish a more permanent camp, Bodniev approached Deborah and Selma and said.

"We are going to take advantage of the first lights to begin the exploration."

"We can wait for Dennis and Jack to finish the setting up the camp." answered Debbie.

"No, neither they nor you will be part of this stage."

"I do not understand you."

"I have thought to invite to Selma to accompany me in the exploration."

"Why Selma?" Debbie looked startled.

"I told you I can sense that your sister has ... special powers. I can detect them every time I'm near her."

"Silly stuff. She never showed those powers before."

At that time, Selma got into the discussion on a topic that directly concerned her.

"You do not really know my perceptions. You do not know what I feel at certain times. You only know what I tell you."

The older sister looked completely bewildered. Then she resumed his aplomb and said.

"As your older sister, I feel responsible for you. If you want to go ... so be it, but I will accompany you at all times."

Selma was preparing to respond with an angry gesture when the Russian interposed himself in what seemed to be a difficult argument between sisters. Addressing Debbie he said.

"I agree with you to accompany us but it is necessary that these powers be manifested in Selma, which requires a high degree of concentration and isolation and it is important that you do not interfere in this process. You can come walking behind us at a safe distance. There will come a time when I will separate myself too and let Selma guide us."

Deborah thought for a moment and finally agreed.

"Very well, but I must always have you in sight."

The shaman lowered his arms in a dejected gesture and finally said.

"I agree.".

He then turned to his tent and said.

"I'm going to prepare some equipment. Make sure you bring something to eat and especially water. We will probably be many hours since the valley is extensive."

The three walkers had already traveled a considerable part of the surface of the depression between the hills without any of them finding places that seemed remarkable. As they had been sweeping the valley from one eastern end to the western, they had finally reached one of the edges next to one of the elevations, which was surrounded by rather high rocky crags. Bodniev, fatigued by the walk, sat on one of the rocks and invited Selma to do the same. Then he put his hand in the backpack that always accompanied him, a kind of miraculous bag from which he drew elements as varied as unexpected; Selma watched him absentmindedly without any particular interest. At last the Siberian breathed a sigh of satisfaction as he extracted a bundle of metals and threads that the girl soon recognized.

"You have a special sensitivity with the pendulum." Said the shaman. "It is time to test them directly on the ground."

They both stood up and the young woman took the instrument, letting the steel cone hang down by gravity.

"What should I do?"

"Walk in one consistent directions in the form of a spiral with center in this rock, and we will see if the pendulum sets in motion at some time, or if you register in your body some form of vibrations, even if they do not appear in the device."

The girl began to describe scrolls increasingly distant from the stone taken as a reference with a gesture of great concentration and seriousness. Bodniev watched her closely and the performance confirmed that his previous presumption that Selma had a natural predisposition for dowsing was correct. The activity lasted for half an hour, during which Selma had departed about a hundred meters in diameter from the reference point. Perceiving the fatigue that the girl was already beginning to show, the Russian stood up and walked towards her telling her when he was near.

" Now rest a little, marking the position in which you are."

Selma simply sat on the grassy floor while Bodniev approached her.

" This place is vaguely familiar." expressed the Siberian when arriving. "I have a good feeling."

After restoring forces for a while the young woman stood up again and continued her exploration, while the Russian returned to the rock taken as a starting point. As soon as he was seated in it he looked back at Selma and with surprise saw that she had stopped and looked around the place where she was with a certain bewilderment.

Bodniev stood up again and rushed towards the young woman with unsuspected speed in such a big man, while shouting.

"Stay there. Do not move."

As he approached the place where the girl was waiting for him, the shaman cast a comprehensive glance at the landscape in front of him, the valley, the cordon of surrounding hills and the rocks located closer to them. He felt as if a veil were running in front of his eyes, slowed his fast walk and with signs of excitement he turned 360 degrees around himself.

"This is the place of my visions, I recognize the natural environment perfectly. What have you felt?"

"I do not know exactly, what I experience is a strong directionality towards those dark and large rocks."

"But this is the site of my visions." Insisted the Siberian. Then he began to collect loose stones around and stack them where Selma was.

"Come on, help me build a monolith."

When the pile of stones rose a little less than a meter in height, Bodniev said.

"It's enough. It is visible from far away."

"And now what will we do?"

" We will return with the others bringing shovels and other elements."

They first walked up to the place where Debbie was waiting and then they all returned to the camp.

Dennis, Jack and Martín were cleaning the trucks when they saw the young women and the Russian approaching.

"They look agitated." Dennis said. "Maybe they´ve got news."

Chapter 15

They had loaded all the elements to work in the excavation in one of the trucks and in the other utilitarian vehicle traveled all the members of the expedition except one of the custodians who remained in the camp next to the big truck to watch them.

Soon they saw the monolith erected by Bodniev and Selma and as they arrived at it began to unload the shovels of the vehicles. All the men began to excavate the hard ground that lay under the thin layer of grass, working under the rays of the Sun that soon began to make its effects felt on the diggers. Debbie and Selma had brought water canteens to avoid dehydration of the workers, a risk always present in the dry desert climate.

"How deep do you think we need to dig?" asked Deborah addressing Bodniev.

"No more than four meters, but before reaching that depth we should see signs of some previous activity."

The men were digging holes in a circle about twenty meters in diameter around the monolith. After two hours of work one of the Mongols made signs while uttering some cries addressed to Batbayar.

"There's something there." The guide explained as everyone approached the site. Upon arrival, the custodian indicated the hole in which he was working. Inside it everybody could see stones that were obviously out of place at that depth.

"In this place there has been previous human activity." stated Dennis. "Let's concentrate our efforts in this hole."

The well had grown in diameter and depth and some of the workers had sat on its walls in order to catch a breath. Jack was one of those who kept shoveling when he suddenly exhaled a curse.

"What's wrong, Jack?" asked Debbie obviously scared.

"I've hit something hard."

"Wait. Do not continue. Let's all dig around." said Dennis in a loud voice that denoted his excitement.

When they had deepened around the obstacle that Jack had encountered, Bodniev slid his immense body into the pit and with great effort lifted the object Jack's shovel had hit.

"What the hell is that? It looks like wood." asked Martín with a puzzled expression.

The Russian deposited his load on the ground outside the well while dictating.

"These are the shattered remains of a wooden chest. The dry climate and the absence of rain that would otherwise have penetrated the soil have kept it from rotting."

" So you think it is the remnant of a chest belonging...?" Martín did not dare to complete the question.

"In all likelihood it's part of what Baron Ungern's men buried. Let's continue digging around but carefully so as not to damage other possible remains."

The hours passed marked every so often by exclamations that gave account of the finding of some remains inside the big pit that had notoriously expanded. For a time they continued to be illuminated by the headlights of the vehicles that had been able to approach about fifty meters until that lighting became insufficient. After a while of being only illuminated by the torches and by a waning moon that provided very little visibility to the enlarged hole, Jack said.

" It makes no sense to exhaust the batteries of our flashlights without achieving results. In any case it is obvious that there are no gold or silver ingots here. Let's go back to the camp and we'll come back to this place tomorrow morning."

At dawn of the next day the camp began its activities and a half hour later the two vans arrived at the excavation abandoned the night before. Everything looked clear then. The pit measured about twenty meters in diameter and was about six meters deep, and on its outer edges there were all kinds of objects rescued from the bottom. The travelers settled around the hole and watched in silence until Jack reiterated.

"There is no point in continuing to dig, there is nothing else in this place." He looked around and found that there was consensus.

"Let´s examine what we have found and see what these remains tell us."

They put all the objects in a row on the ground and each of the members took one of them, moved apart and analyzed each object in detail, taking note of his observations. After the task was completed Jack summoned his colleagues to perform an evaluation.

"Well, we have pieces of leather that presumably belonged to baggage, pieces of thick cloth and some pieces of torn metal. What does all this tell us?" The question was a challenge to the imagination of all the expedition members.

A momentary silence prevailed until Dennis raised his hand.

"Yes, Dennis." conceded Jack.

"All these objects belong to packaging of different materials and sizes, from which the content was removed and were later discarded. It is evident that, if this is indeed the place where the men of Baron von Ungern buried the treasure, someone came afterwards and withdrew it. Someone who knew precisely where to look."

Next, Debbie spoke.

"Although there are enough pieces of packaging material, it seems to me to be too few for something that was considered the treasure of Outer Mongolia. I think these were opened only to verify that it was indeed what the looters were looking for and once confirmed, they took the rest with their packaging, which otherwise is more logical than leaving it here."

A murmur of approval followed her words.

Then it was Martín's turn.

"I wonder why they have placed these remains in the place where we found them and took the trouble to cover the well again, when they could have left everything out in the open."

"And do you have an answer for your own question?"

"The obvious one is that they wanted to erase their traces."

"... because the knowledge that the treasure had been looted would indicate that it was removed by those who had buried it, since they were the only ones who knew its location. This would directly point at them as the looters. This is like a crime where they have made the body disappear." Debbie completed the hint.

"I can only add that this is without a doubt the place where the events that my visions showed took place. It's just as I remember it." Said the shaman.

" It is fair to recognize that without the visions of Aman we would never have found this place and the secret of the looters would have remained forever unknown." admitted Jack, and then addressing the Russian." The accuracy of your predictions is remarkable."

"Well, someone else? Where is Selma?

"Where is my sister? "repeated alarmed Debbie.

"I saw her go in that direction, toward those rocks." announced Martín." She had B's pendulum in her hands.

The Russian patted his forehead.

"Now I remember that when I recognized this place Selma insisted that the pendulum vibrations were pointing in another direction. Precisely towards those big rocks."

"Let's go find her." said Dennis. "You Batbayar, stay with your men to control this place."

Debbie, Dennis, Jack, Bodniev and Martín headed for the cliff, some two hundred meters distant.

"Selma is not anywhere at sight." sobbed obviously anguished Deborah. "I should have never agreed to bring my little sister to this place."

"Don't torture yourself." answered Dennis taking her in his arms. This valley is a safe place. She will appear safe."

"Let's split and surround the rocks. We'll find her somewhere."

For a half hour they were looking for the girl while the degree of anxiety grew and not just in Debbie. Finally, after turning around the outcrop, they found themselves facing the rock again.

"Where is Martín?" Dennis asked. "The last thing we need is another member gone astray."

At that moment a voice was heard from a higher place of the mountain. Martín had climbed a fairly steep slope and was signaling them from about thirty meters above their level.

"Have you found her?" asked Debbie in a broken voice.

"I think that these bushes here that have been moved recently." shouted the boy. There is a kind of entrance to a cave or something.

"Stay there and wait for us. Do not move." said aloud his relative also. Then he told Jack. "The two of us will go up and join him."

"All right. Just let me go to the truck to look for flashlights and ropes. If it really is a cave we'll need them."

At that moment Tsegseg showed up; the girl had been present but remained in the background during the entire event. Approaching the base of the hill she began to climb it jumping the crags and avoiding the pitfalls that the rugged cliff offered at a breathtaking speed as if her feet were endowed with wings that allowed her to move where others would have needed to cling to the roughness of the rock. She finally reached the place where Martín was waiting.

Everyone from below looked at her in amazement.

"Who is really this girl? Not even a mountain goat could have climbed the cliff in that way." asked Dennis completely bewildered.

"I had heard that her ancestors could walk in the mountains." said in an excited voice Batbayar, who had joined the group. "But I had really never witnessed it. Moreover, I always had doubts about the veracity of those old stories."

"What stories and what ancestors are you talking about, Batbayar? " Asked Jack, who could not get out of his astonishment.

"I think I've talked too much." replied the Mongol, and immediately disappeared to join his men who had looked at the event from a certain distance and were in a reclusive attitude as if they were in a religious ceremony.

Martín, who could not leave his stupor, moved away from where he was, letting Tsegseg watch at what actually looked like the entrance to a cave that went deep into the hill. The young Mongol woman passed by him and without a second of hesitation entered into the bowels of the mysterious tunnel. There was no light in the enclosure she had entered so that the boy did not understand what was guiding her steps but following an impulse that pushed him every time Tsegseg made her appearance he ran after her, trying to walk safely in the interior by feeling the walls of the cavity.

When Dennis and Jack managed to reach the entrance to the tunnel it was thus deserted. Each of the men held a powerful electric torch and left the rest of the gear they had brought on the entrance floor, including ropes and hooks. The two advanced along what proved to be a real cavern that extended by dozens of steps in the belly of the mountain following tortuous courses.

"I wonder what forces have dug this tunnel and how it happened." wondered Dennis.

"I think only water could have drilled the mountain in this way." answered Jack.

" Water in this desert? Flowing at the speed that is necessary to pierce the stone? And about thirty meters above the level of the surrounding desert?"

"Maybe this was not always a desert and maybe it was not always at this height. Certain deserts have been sea beds in other geological eras."

At that moment a breeze from the inside reached his face and a certain luminosity could be seen in front of them.

THE GOBI CODEX- LOST TREASUREBEYON A FLEEING HORIZON

What they saw after turning the following bend in the path left them completely astonished. The narrow internal corridor they had followed suddenly widened to the dimensions of a vast natural room, illuminated by a kind of roof top opening through which air and light entered. Selma, Tsegseg and Martín were standing in front of a long horizontal rock that ran through the place from end to end. On it lay a number of pieces that reflected with a golden glow the indirect light they received.

The three young people were in a respectful position in front of the findings. Selma and Martín turned their faces to look at the two newcomers. Tsegseg stepped forward and placed her hand on the stone. At the moment when her fingers came into contact with one of the metal bars, the outline of the girl's body lit up with a glow that dazzled her companions at first.

Obeying some strange impulse, Martín approached the young woman and placed his own hand on hers. No effect followed his action.

Chapter 16

Selma covered her face, while Jack and Dennis could not come out of amazement produced by the disturbing fact.

The girl was in an altered emotional state and her look seemed lost; she was still holding in her left hand the pendulum that oscillated visibly; everybody realized that it was once more the artifact that had driven her there. Jack took the young woman by the arm and led her to the entrance of the hall and then to the corridors they had crossed to get there. As he passed next Dennis, he muttered.

"She is in a state of hypnotic trance perhaps induced by her use of the pendulum. I'm going to take her outdoors."

"I think I need it, too."

"Are you going to leave Martín alone with that girl?"

"I do not think he needs me, not even that he realizes I'm here."

When they reached the entrance to the cave they met Batbayar, who had also undergone a change in his look, visible in his clothing. He wore an oriental warrior outfit and wore a strange scimitar hanging from his waist, an unexpected artifact in the 21st century.

"What are you doing here?" asked Dennis, who was receiving one surprise after another"

"What I've done in recent years. Protect the princess."

" You mean Tsegseg?"

"Yes".

" You will enter the cave?

"No, unless it is necessary."

Completely confused Dennis followed Jack and between them led Selma down the hill.

Martín was standing next to Tsegseg, aware of the girl's minimal movements. She stared at the gold ingots that lay carefully placed on the rough surface of the stone. Finally the woman turned her face looking at him and Martín could see a strange glint in her eyes. Her small hand rested on his arm and then she led him to a corner of the wide room that still remained in the darkness. There the girl began to undress and with her head indicated him to do the same.

They both lay on the floor and when they reached the climax together, Martín realized that he was part of a religious ritual whose meaning and consequences he could not understand.

The girl turned to one side; on her lips a smile had appeared that she wanted to keep hidden. In that afternoon she had achieved two fundamental goals in her life. On the one hand she had found the treasure of her people and on the other she had been fertilized in a sacred place. In her inner circle, Tsegseg knew that the son she was going to conceive would lead her people to freedom.

It was already dark by the time they arrived at the place where they had left the two vehicles. They all looked fatigued and confused. Dennis lit a precarious fire with scattered branches and herbs in which Debbie heated the food they had brought. Jack intended to ask Bodniev some questions but the Russian stopped him with a sign of his right hand.

"For now I have no answers. You have to let the night decant and my ideas settle down." He said.

They ate in silence and when they had finished they saw Tsegseg accompanied by Martín and Batbayar in the dim light of the waning moon.

"I think it best to return to the camp to spend the night in tents and sleeping bags. Tomorrow we can return once more to this place."

They traveled in the light of the van headlight and found that the Mongol guards had lit a good fire. Tsegseg, Selma and Martín went each to his tent because they had had an exhausting day due to the tension they had been subjected to. The Mongols remained in their place, while the others, although they were fatigued, could not fall asleep and preferred to be part of a meeting around the bonfire until late. Bodniev invited Batbayar to join the group.

"I THINK WE CAN TRY to find some sense, even partial, t said Dennis, interpreting the general feeling.

"It seems right to me, you can start yourself." answered Jack.

"All right. The extraordinary events began with the confirmation that the treasure -which I previously believed was only an oriental myth- really exists, although it is not of the magnitude of the tale. The fact that it was not in the place indicated by Aman but in a nearby one is perhaps explained by hypothesizing that one of Baron von Ungern´s henchmen returned in order to relocate it safely in a place ignored by the rest of his comrades who had originally carried it."

"We have been able to find it due to two separate paranormal events." added Jack.

" On the one hand, Aman led us here guided by his visions, but we also needed the intervention of Selma and the pendulum to find the true location."

"It is true, we have found the treasure by the extremely unlikely concurrence of two paranormal facts." Concluded Deborah.

Bodniev, who had remained silent until then, addressed the guide in a serious tone.

"Tell us, Batbayar, but this time tell us the whole story. Who are you and who is really Tsegseg? Is she just the daughter of a Mongol chieftain among so many others or is it someone else?"

The usually modest guide stood up, wearing the uniform he had previously displayed on the mountain. His gesture was haughty. After everything that had happened in front of the cave and inside it, he knew that he could no longer deceive his traveling companions, in particular the Siberian shaman, who knew all the secrets of Central Asia.

"Tsegseg is indeed the daughter of the current leader of the Mongolian tribes, but at the same time a direct descendant of Bogd Khan."

"Ungern von Sternberg´s puppet King." exclaimed Jack.

"That is the Euro-centric vision of the fact." answered proudly Batbayar. "The truth is that Bogd Khan used Baron von Ungern and his military genius to drive the Chinese out, to keep the Russian Bolsheviks at bay and reconstitute the Mongol monarchy. But that is not all that the genealogy teaches us."

"What do you mean?"

"Bogd Khan was a descendant of Genghis Khan himself. That is why the tribes submitted to him."

A silence of stupor followed this revelation.

" Returning to my original question." Added Bodniev." This means that Tsegseg herself descends from the great Genghis Khan."

"That is her ancestry by paternal line. But even more significant is her maternal ancestry."

Everyone was waiting for the Mongol to continue his narrative.

"The Princess Tsegseg is the daughter of the highest priestess of Tengrism."

"The shamanic and animistic religion of the Mongolian tribes." Explained Bodniev. Then went on. "It is a ritual that mixes traditional shamanism with Buddhism."

"That is the Yellow Tengrism." replied Batbayar." But Tsegseg´s mother belongs to the branch of black Tengrism, the true original religion of the Mongol people."

Involuntarily Bodniev let out an exhale.

"What happens?" asked Jack.

"It is an ancestral ritual, whose referent is precisely Genghis Khan, who for his followers was an incarnation of the gods. This rite is directly related to magic."

"What implications has that Tsegseg´s maternal ascendancy?" asked Dennis addressing Batbayar.

"The princess has inherited all the powers of her predecessors, transmitted by the *udgan,* i.e. the priestesses, to their eldest daughters."

"Does that include magical powers?" inquired Debbie.

"Not only magical." Although the question was not intended for him, Bodniev anticipated answering. "Also the possibility of involuntarily provoking certain hypnotic trances and inducing visions in the attendees."

"Do you mean that what we have witnessed, Tsegseg literally walking up the hill slope... her transfiguration on the altar covered with gold ingots ...?" Deborah looked bewildered.

"We do not know if it happened in reality or only in our perceptions." completed the Russian with his deep voice. Then he went back to Batbayar. "Could you talk to Tsegseg after the discovery?"

"Briefly."

"What did she tell you, for example about the gold?"

" It's just part of the original treasure. We do not know what happened with the rest."

"You have not answered part of our original question." observed Jack. "Who are you really?"

" You would say that I am the seneschal of the court of the Kingdom of Mongolia."

" Where is that court?"

"Dispersed in the huge Mongolian territory. Everywhere and nowhere."

"It´s impossible to obtain precisions in all this subject. We can never reach to hard facts" said resignedly Dennis.

"It belongs to a sphere other than what you know as concrete reality." replied Bodniev. "A foggy sphere that is between wakefulness and dreams, but no less real."

"Well, I propose that we leave this conversation for tonight." said Jack." Tomorrow early we will go back to the cave and we will make an inventory of what is in it."

Chapter 17

After a frugal breakfast the travelers rode in the two vans and started the short trip they had already made the day before. Batbayar was driving a vehicle carrying Tsegseg, Martín and Jack, while in the other Dennis was carrying Deborah, Selma and Bodniev. The Mongol custodians were left to take care of the camp, but in reality Batbayar did not want them to witness the events that would eventually happen.

When they arrived at the site where the pit had been dug the previous day and according to what had been previously agreed, the explorers proceeded to cover it and tamp the soil, so time would again cover all traces of its existence as had happened before. The wrappers that had once contained ingots and which they had scattered around were lifted and carried away by the travelers on their new ascent of the hill to leave them inside the cave. Dennis was the first to reach the mouth of the cavern and lighting his flashlight led the way through the corridors that were already familiar to them. Finally they reached the overhead illuminated area and could appreciate that with the morning light it looked different than what they remembered.

Jack and Dennis escorted by Batbayar who had entered the cave this time, were counting the existing gold bars, documenting all their findings in Dennis's notebook on an Excel spreadsheet and at the same time registering them with a video camera. It was clear that the real function of the person who had joined the expedition as a guide was that of auditor and guarantor of the integrity of the proceedings on behalf of the Mongol government in the shadows, which claimed to be the successor to Bogd Khan. The true heiress in a genetic sense, Tsegseg, contemplated everything from a corner of the wide room with a dreamlike aspect. Debbie, Selma and Martín toured every corner of the room and the innumerable side corridors and recesses that in past times the action of water had carved into the sandstone that formed the interior of the hill. Bodniev had sat on a large stone and was in a meditative pose.

THE GOBI CODEX- LOST TREASURE BEYON A FLEEING HORIZON

"Debbie, Martín! Come see this." Selma's voice propagated by echo came from one of the corridors that opened to the left. The tone was imperative.

The aforementioned approached somewhat alarmed, followed by the Russian. At the end of the corridor, the young woman was standing in front of another flat rock, on which they could see a series of dust covered bundles.

"They are like backpacks or bags." Martín was counting the number of objects. "There are twelve in total. Then he stretched out a hand to take the object farther to the right."

"Wait." Debbie stopped him suddenly. "I'll call Dennis and he will film the whole scene just as we found it."

Bodniev approached Selma with a smile on his lips. He spoke in a very low voice so that only the girl could hear him.

" As I always supposed, it is you who finally make all the findings. I know that you still are not entirely convinced but there is no doubt that you have a very highly developed and infrequent sensitivity. It is a gift that you must recognize and cultivate but you need in the first steps the guidance of a clairvoyant. I can help you in this task if you want it."

Once the metallic treasure inventory was finished, the action was moved to the side aisle. In total, there were twelve thick canvas backpacks, which time and dryness had turned brittle, but which proved effective in preserving their content. Jack was in charge of opening the bags one by one and arranging them on the surface of the rock that served as a table, while Debbie and Dennis proceeded to film and document everything found. These were old documents written in Cyrillic, Chinese and in the Mongolian alphabet, with its complicated vertically developed characters filled with volutes and dots. Many of the documents were folded and sealed with official stamps of unknown origin. Only Jack manipulated the incunabula and did it with gloves and using great caution to prevent the paper from being reduced to dust. In addition to the filming made by his relative, Martín was photographing each of the documents using the camera on his cell phone to have a backup copy of all the documentation. Everyone was focused on their task and there was silence in the room. Attentive to his role as a witness, Batbayar contemplated everything from a prudent distance without interfering in the works.

Bodniev had put on unsuspected glasses that he had extracted from his infinite backpack and was examining the pages closely without touching them. Finally he expressed.

"Some of them are official documents of Mongol origin, coming from the period in which the monarchy had been restored, that is to say, the time of Bogd Khan and Baron von Ungern. Others are Chinese papers of which I cannot give details and finally there are Russian documents from the Czarist era that I would like to be able to analyze in detail later. I think all this comes from the first twenty years of the twentieth century."

"It is the official documentation of the Kingdom of Mongolia that Bogd Khan tried to save before the advance of the communists who put an end to that kingdom and kept the Khan captive." argued Batbayar with surprising knowledge." These documents are an essential part of the treasure that we are looking for and thus belong to our historical heritage."

Tsegseg left her absent state and approached to observe the findings with obvious interest. She read the documents in Mongolian in a low voice and made some comments in that language with her custodian Batbayar. Finally she said

" In the name of the Kingdom of Mongolia and as its legitimate representative I claim the possession of this treasure for my people."

The expression had no immediate response. Dennis approached Jack and asked him.

" Do you know if Bluthund has any position taken on this aspect?"

" A priori I would say that the general position is to grant possession to the legitimate owners. But we really need to confirm it tonight on the radio with my contacts in New York. In short, they are the ones who have sponsored and financed this expedition and it is fair that they decide on the fate of the findings."

Once again Selma gave a voice of alarm drawing everyone's attention. She had climbed over some rocky ledges until she reached a hole in the wall that turned out to be a kind of niche.

"There's something else here." She said to Jack. "Maybe you want to extract it yourself."

When the man placed the contents on the rock and untied the canvas wrapper, they could visualize three very damaged books with red leather covers. Dennis approached to film them while Jack turned the pages one by one to allow the individual registration. The books were hand-written with blue ink, with careful calligraphy evidencing that they were the work of only one hand. Finally Dennis said in a low voice.

"These are the diaries of Baron Ungern von Sternberg."

Jack emerged from the tent where he had been talking on the radio with his contacts in New York. Hours earlier, the man had communicated the findings detailing their content. The interlocutors had said that they would call him later to give instructions after discussing the issue in a plenary of the Bluthund Community leaders. Finally the call came and the man summoned his close group, formed by Debbie, Selma, Dennis, Martín and in this case he added Bodniev to them.

"The instructions are clear and agree with the precedents I know." He paused and continued.

"They have confirmed Tsegseg's identity. The girl is who she says she is and also Batbayar. We have to give them the metallic treasure and the official documents of Bogd Khan's period of government, but we will keep Baron von Ungern's diaries with us and will take them to

New York. The members of Bluthund who have contact with Tsegseg's father will arrange with him a compensation that the Mongols must make to cover the expenses of the expedition. My contacts seem to be much more interested in those diaries than in the rest. In any case they were not part of the Mongolian treasure but von Ungern added them to be put in a safe place before being shot by the Bolsheviks. They are not part of the Mongolian heritage. Now let's talk with Tsegseg and Batbayar."

"I am relieved that we can give satisfaction to your requests" Dennis said referring to the last mentioned ones.

"What do you mean?"

"I do not know what their reaction would have been if we wanted to dispute her treasure. Do not forget that they have several armed men under Batbayar's direction."

Chapter 18

The discussion with Tsegseg and Batbayar about the division of the elements found in the cave was brief and friendly. In fact, the Mongols kept all the metallic components and all documentation whose origin was unmistakably Mongolian. On the opposite side Baron von Ungern von Sternberg had played an important role in the life of the country but only during an ephemeral period. In addition, ultimately, despite his eccentric passion for Lamaism and Buddhism, he was a European and his diaries would not have much value for the current descendants of Bogd Khan.

The negotiations were done by Jack and Dennis on the side of the members of the Bluthund Community and Batbayar with the silent presence of Tsegseg by the Mongols.

"Our purpose in this spot has been fulfilled and now we must prepare the return to Ulan Bator." said Dennis." This involves going through the Gobi Desert in the opposite direction until arriving at the trans-Mongolian railway station. We are going to take the diaries of Baron von Ungern with us but I ask you what do you plan to do with the gold bars and the documents? The latter are very fragile and will not stand a hazardous journey through the desert."

"Princess Tsegseg, my men and I are going to stay in this place, with the exception of a guide who will take you through the desert." answered Batbayar." This guide speaks a little Russian and Bodniev and he can understand each other perfectly well."

"We cannot simply abandon you in this wasteland." answered Dennis." Can we communicate by radio with someone to come and look for you? In that case we would wait for their arrival."

"The Princess has already communicated with her mother and the help is already on the way." was the unexpected response.

Jack and Dennis looked at each other perplexed but they were already accustomed to the surprises given by the skills of the young Mongolian. Then they completed the negotiations agreeing the subdivision of the elements of the expedition and went with their literary booty towards the camp. There they informed their colleagues about the decision.

"What does it mean that Tsegseg communicated with her mother?" Asked incredulous Deborah. " By telepathy?"

"The shamans of Central Asia assiduously practice telepathy or extra-sensorial communication, as well as travel through space and time in their dreams." explained Bodniev.

" Even a positivist like Freud had to admit that telepathy is something possible." added Debbie. "He apparently found experiences of that type in his studies."

"It is a more likely phenomenon among clairvoyants and among people who are closely related, such as Tsegseg and her mother." explained the Russian. "I have not had personal experiences of that type but I do know undoubted cases of extrasensory communication between members of Siberian tribes."

Preparations for the trip took all the rest of the day. Once his part of the tasks was completed Martín said he was going to say goodbye to Tsegseg, since the woman had not planned to leave the cave at all. He walked from the camp to the hill where she was and climbed the steep slope. Upon reaching the vast enclosure where they had found the treasure, the boy visualized Tsegseg and her custodian sitting on the rock. Discreetly Batbayar retreated to the entrance of the cave to provide intimacy to the two young people.

The prolonged meeting was totally silent. Martín sat at the girl's feet and took her right hand in his. Tsegseg was looking hieratically forward like an Egyptian Goddess. The young man felt his mind was being explored by an external power, but the contact was ethereal, pleasant and without violence. Martín realized that various thoughts were being recorded in his psyche and lent himself passively to the experience, without attempting to challenge it or answer the thoughts. Finally he rose and kissed the girl's forehead; only then did he realize that Tsegseg was surrounded by a strange golden glow, which he did not know if it was real or simply a sensory experience. He walked to the exit of the room without turning back while a smile lit his face. He crossed with Batbayar to the exit of the cavern and began the descent of the slope. Meanwhile the contents received in the silent meeting with Tsegseg paraded through his mind. The girl would return to her world to fulfill her destiny. There she would give birth to their son and educate him to take charge of the destinies of the Mongolian people. The treasures found would be applied to the service of that cause. The last thought transmitted by the young woman was the most flattering. Tsegseg would call him, Martín, to join her when circumstances were propitious.

The next morning the expedition started back to its starting point. A trip of between two and three days on the sand was waiting them. At nightfall on the first day they came across a long line of Mongolian horsemen traveling in the opposite direction. The custodian who accompanied them, a very silent man, voiced something out loud that Bodniev translated.

"These are the warriors who are going to escort Lady Tsegseg and the treasure of her people."

On the night of the second day they finally arrived at the Chojr station, from where they had departed twenty-two days before. The place was completely dark and they had to wait fifteen hours for the next train to return to Ulan Bator and from there travel back to Moscow first and then to New York by means of two Aeroflot flights.

The following morning Bodniev said goodbye in the same austere and mysterious manner in which he had previously appeared at the station.

"How will you return home?" asked Dennis. "How will you travel from this remote station in Mongolia?"

"The same way I arrived." It was the laconic and enigmatic answer.

As they watched him go Debbie said.

"It hurts me to see Aman go like this, after everything we've shared, dangers and successes. It is unlikely that we will see him again. We do not even know where he lives, in what town his house is."

"What is it that led him to collaborate with us?" Reflected Dennis." Will Bluthund reward him in any way?"

"I do not know." Jack confessed frankly. "The community we call that name recruits its followers in very varied terms and strange ways."

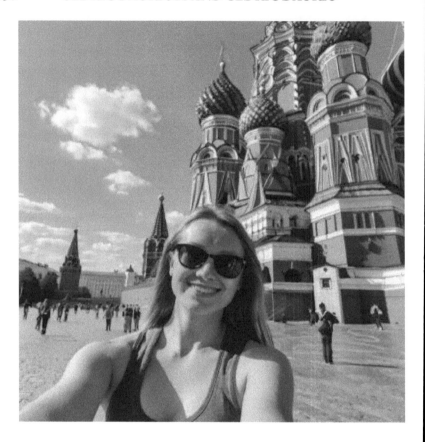

They decided to spend a day in Moscow before starting the trip back to New York in order to rest and relax the nervous and muscular tension they had accumulated for the period of almost a month. While Deborah, Selma, Dennis and Martín made a series of customary sightseeing in the Russian capital, Jack stayed at the hotel trying to make contact with his counterparts in Bluthund.

When at approximately 7:00 p.m. the travelers returned they found their companion having a drink in solitude in the bar attached to the hotel. His face showed good humor.

"Can we sit with you?" asked Debbie.

"Of course, but not here at the bar. Come, there is an empty table at the restaurant."

For half an hour the newcomers were sharing impressions and memories and exhibiting photos of the sites they had visited.

"And what do you say? " Asked Debbie. "You look happy."

"First I could rest, which I needed more than I imagined."

"And is that all you have to tell?

"No." Jack paused to stimulate the curiosity of the others.

"Well, spit it out!" urged Dennis.

"I had a long talk with my contact, in which I described the material of Baron von Ungern's diaries. I could not give many details because although some parts are written in German, which as you know I understand, most of it is in Russian, especially the last part."

"So?"

"I was forced to scan several sections at random and send the information. An hour later they called me again. It seems that the material interests them a lot. I think they are even more interested than they were in Bogd Khan's treasure, which was what originally took us to Central Asia."

" How is that possible? " The one who carried the lead in the questions was Dennis.

"I do not know with certainty, but it is evident that von Ungern's notebooks have touched a very sensitive fiber of our friends, more than a simple treasure in precious metals. We will find out when we arrive. They have planned a meeting for the day after tomorrow, but only with me since in it I will hand over von Ungern's diaries, the photos and filming obtained and my notes. Once they have been analyzed, a plenary meeting will be held with all the members of the expedition."

Chapter 19

Some of them were for the first time in the spacious meeting room located in the headquarters of a major international investment bank, whose CEO was one of the leading figures of the Bluthund Community. Only Jack had already been at the meeting place, when he had attended as a simple assistant and not as a central figure as in that opportunity. Deborah, Selma, Dennis and Martín had delegated to him the responsibility of being the reporting member of the expedition. While Debbie and Dennis, regular participants in executive meetings in other media, felt self assured and self-confident, the two young people looked somewhat inhibited. Selma was accustomed to being in luxurious surroundings due to her family relationships, but the austere and solemn atmosphere of the room with boiserie-covered walls, pictures of august characters, no doubt founders of the company in distant times, as well as other landscape paintings of undoubted pictorial value produced a deep psychological impact in her, which undoubtedly was the function by which they were in the place. As for Martín, the whole experience was strange and alien to him.

Around the vast table sat a score of characters of serious and silent aspect, among which were people of both sexes and belonging to all ethnic groups on Earth. All of them were carefully dressed, most of the men in suits of the most expensive tailors of the planet while the women gave the note of color and variety with typical attires of their countries of origin. There was no doubt that the Bluthund Community was proud of its diversity and power and wore them with splendor but without vanity or arrogance.

As he sat in the chair that a kind of master of ceremonies indicated to him, Martín had an infrequent feeling of misplacement due to his modest clothing, which included jeans and slippers and a jacket lent by his relative, which was quite large. He compared himself not with the rest of the attendees but with his fellow adventurers, all those who were up to the circumstances, and in the case of the two women, dazzling. In particular he observed Selma and had to suppress a gesture of admiration. The girl was without dispute the most beautiful woman in the room and that day he saw her with new eyes, realizing that she was a shining star in the demanding New York scenario. Martín could not hide his pride in being friends with the young woman.

Deborah looked at her sister with a serene attitude of complacency, as she also perceived that Selma was a focus of visual attraction in the large room populated by important people from around the world. Then she looked at Dennis who seemed somewhat uncomfortable with his tie and both exchanged non-verbal messages. The man then glanced at Selma and opened his eyes in admiration.

The girl was going through an ambiguous moment, mixing satisfaction with the impact she knew she was causing with a little embarrassment that the environment produced in her. Deep inside she knew that she cared about the judgments of all those personalities but above all the admiration of the young man who was sitting in front of her trying to hide his jeans and shoes. Selma did not deceive herself about her own feelings and knew that in reality she had dressed to shock the boy and erase the image of Tsegseg from his impressionable mind.

One of the older characters, seated at the head of the table, gently tapped the water glass in front of him with a teaspoon as he stood up. The master of ceremonies, a man named Watkins, exclaimed loudly.

"Our Master, Dr. Richardson, is going to speak."

The man named Richardson began to speak in excellent English, in a persuasive tone and with great expository coherence as well as with great simplicity. He made a summary of the objectives of the expedition, the organizational aspects, the resources employed, and made a presentation of the members including those present and Bodniev, whom he mentioned as an expert in traditional Siberian healing arts. He also mentioned those he called representatives of the "alternative government" of Mongolia.

The Master then gave the floor to Jack Berglund, whom he described as "one of the most outstanding organizers of confidential research in our Community."

Jack gave a detailed account of the course of the expedition, giving colorful descriptions of the sites visited, the windstorms of the desert, the attack of the Mongol bandits and the discovery of the site sought by the visions of Bodniev. Then he related the determination of the location of the cavern thanks to the "special gifts" of our companion, pointing to Selma who blushed when she felt all the gazes placed on her this time not because of her looks but her achievements.

Jack approached a screen placed on the side of the table and visible to all while Dennis , who was placed next to a projection equipment at a signal put it into operation. Both men showed all the filmic and photographic material produced in the expedition which had been edited by Bluthund specialists to give continuity and unity. Obviously the exhibitors had previously agreed what part of the material would be explained by each one, with Dennis focusing on the technical issues and Jack on the significance of the findings. As expected, the films that exhibited the gold ingots attracted the utmost attention. When they showed the stamps engraved on the ingots, Dr. Richardson asked them to stop and approached the screen in order to examine the images better. At the end they projected a series of photos of Baron von Ungern's diaries.

At the end they answered a long series of questions made by the assistants, and when it became evident that the doubts were exhausted they sat down. As a sign of approval, Deborah placed a hand on her boyfriend's..

Dr. Richardson stood up again and thanked the exhibitors for their didactic clarity and all the members of the expedition for their efforts and dedication. He then explained the distribution of the treasure between the representatives of the Mongolian government in exile and the Community. He finished his speech by saying.

"But these are these notebooks or diaries in which Baron Ungern von Sternberg narrated all his experiences that are worthy of our maximum attention. The Baron was one of the most extraordinary characters that crossed Siberia and Central Asia in the XXth Century and that changed with his courage and military organizational capacity the course of the history of enormous geographical areas of the region. We have asked for the analysis of this material, which is written in German and Russian to one of the greatest exponents on the subject of exo and esoteric Asian knowledge and Western occultism, Dr. Dieter von Eichemberg. Let me invite Dr. Eichemberg to present his conclusions before us."

An imposing personage stood up and approached him, Dr. Richardson shook his hand and sat at his desk at the head of the table.

von Eichemberg was a man of about forty-five, very tall and thin, with blond hair and beard that contrasted with the obvious Eurasian features of his face. He spoke an academic English with a slight Germanic accent. After thanking the attendees, he directly entered the subject.

" Baron Román Ungern von Sternberg was an extraordinary character from several points of view, not all praiseworthy. Noble Russian of German descent born in the Baltic countries, he was commander of Cossack troops in the Russian Imperial Army. After the Russian Revolution he was one of the leaders of the White Movement in the civil war that followed the seizure of power by the Bolsheviks and became a warlord in Central Asia, a dictator of Mongolia in 1921 and exercised his power until he was captured and executed by the Soviets. But it is not due to his military gifts that we are interested in him in this moment, but because of his complex and contradictory political, religious and ... philosophical beliefs, if we can call them that"

Eichenberg paused and watched his audience seeing that he had captured their interest. He then continued.

" In political matters he followed the guidelines of his Tsarist mentors, favoring monarchical and imperial restorations both in Russia and in Mongolia. He was fiercely anti-Semitic and subscribed the pamphlet called "The Protocols of the Elders of Zion" designed by the Tsarist police to justify the pogroms and in general the persecution against the Jews, which served as antecedents to the infamous Nazi racial politics." He then made a stop to emphasize his words.

"We will now turn to his religious believes."

He paused again to sort out his ideas.

"Although raised as a Lutheran from a young age, he showed interest in Eastern religions and mysticism, particularly the more esoteric variants of Lamaism and Buddhism. He pretended to be a reincarnation of Genghis Khan although we do not know if he was really convinced of this nonsense or if he used it to get the Mongol masses to follow him. For the XIII Dalai Lama of Tibet actually von Ungern was by his tendencies the incarnation of a god of destruction, while he considered himself a Mahakala, or a protective deity of

THE GOBI CODEX- LOST TREASURE BEYON A FLEEING HORIZON

Tibetan Vajrayana Buddhism, and it is precisely this connection with Tibet and not with Mongolia the one that interests us now."

"So The Baron was connected to Tantrism, Tibetan Buddhism?" asked an elegant lady.

" That's right, ma'am. It is for that reason that this issue touches me closely ... for family reasons." answered enigmatically von Eichenberg. He took a sip of water and went on.

"To interpret a contradictory figure as von Ungern we have to understand how his subordinates saw him. Indeed, for them, their leader was not only a military genius but also a kind of mystic warrior. Something like a crusader from whom he also said he descended. That explains his lack of compunctions in shedding blood, as he believed he did it for transcendent reasons."

Eichenberg took another sip of water.

"Well." He continued, "We were talking about the relationship with Tibetan Buddhism. von Ungern came to offer his services in writing to the Dalai Lama, an endeavor he did not have the chance to put into practice because he was shot before. But his contemporaries describe him always surrounded by Tibetan lamas and fortunetellers without whom he did not make any military decision. Indeed they were the ones who told him when to move forward and when to back up. Apparently it was also those who recommended him to re-enter Siberian territory, which led to his capture and execution."

New pause and then the speaker added.

"Very well, all this explanation was intended to give you a semblance of our character and its numerous and contradictory facets. We will now narrate the contents of his diary, that is, the three notebooks where he wrote his memories and his daily experiences."

Tibet

Chapter 20

"Before showing you some of the most relevant paragraphs of Baron von Ungern's diary, I will introduce you to the subject to which he repeatedly refers. But let me ask you a question before. What do you associate with the names of Agartha or Shambala?"

The unexpected question generated a moment of confusion among the attendees, until Dr. Richardson expressed.

" In my mind they are linked to confusing legends of oriental origin brought to the West in the early twentieth century by occultists of various kinds ... generally referred to underground cities populated by pure and wise beings of high moral and technological level. Something bordering on utopia and trickery."

"If I'm not mistaken, some Nazi esotericists worked with those traditions before the start of World War II." added a distinguished-looking lady.

Von Eichenberg nodded and said.

"All that is true. References to gigantic tunnel systems connecting underground cities with millions of inhabitants who would enjoy high levels of wisdom are common in the circles of certain branches of Tibetan Buddhism, and extend to Mongolia, Nepal, Tibet, northern India and even to China. The inhabitants of these cities would be practically immortal and would live in diffuse intermediate realms that would exist between our world and another time. According to the myths there are access doors to these tunnels that would be at the same time portals of alternative realities. Really all very confusing and totally opposed to Western positivist thinking."

"And also suggestive and challenging." Said the lady.

" But although the Nazis did not discard all those oriental chimeras, other subjects were of interest to them." Continued von Eichenberg. "The hypothesis of the hollow Earth, however crazy it may sound today, was part of the visions of the official occultists of the Third Reich, who had Himmler and Hitler among their disciples. But more than seats of advanced civilizations they believed that the tunnels had been the cradle of the Aryan race that in those places had developed to the conjuring of the *vril* or vital force and that from there that race had arisen with unstoppable energy to conquer the world and subdue the inferior races."

New pause of Eichenberg in his speech.

"In 1938 a scientist named Ernst Schäffer led a multidisciplinary expedition in Tibet to make anthropometric measurements of the current inhabitants and determine if among them, particularly among the ruling classes, there were traces of those distant ancestors of the Aryans. Another objective was to resume contact with the *vril* to insufflate new energy into the current Europeans."

And in almost inaudible voice added to himself.

"I have personal record of those activities."

The enigmatic phrase was not heard by the audience. Von Eichenberg took a breath and finally said.

"This is the historical context of the issue of cities such as Agartha or its oriental substitute Shambala. Let's see now how Baron von Ungern's diaries are related to that matter."

Said this Eichenberg approached the screen on which Jack Berglund shortly before had exhibited his filmic material. Dennis began with the projection of a Power Point presentation made in a very professional way.

"What I will do is display photos of some pages of the Baron notebooks, generally written in German or Russian, and then their translations into English."

The first of the pages was written in German, with a very neat and even gothic calligraphy, which at the same time gave clues to von Ungern's obsessive features. Dennis then displayed the English translation written in Word. The relevant parts of the text were highlighted in yellow.

"This was written in 1919. "Said Eichenberg. " Please read this sentence."Today I received two Tibetan lamas, sent by the Dalai Lama to probe my attitude towards them. They told me about a very old and wise colleague who has been inside the tunnels that once led to Shambala, and that were later totally or partially blocked by landslides caused by earthquakes in the mountains." "

"This is the first reference that von Ungern makes to concrete contacts with people who had been in the underground world. For several years before he had shown interest in the subject, but with loose unconnected phrases. Please, Dennis, the next slide."

"Today I wrote to the Dalai Lama offering my sword and my horsemen to his service. I sent the letter through a wandering lama, I await his response."

"Next please."

"Two Japanese agents undoubtedly sent by their Emperor came to offer contingents of infantry for our resistance against Russians and Chinese, no doubt believing that they will be able to manipulate me to their liking, but in reality I am going to use them for our cause. I will not let the little yellow men take contact with the *vril* or with the cradle of our race. "

"As you will see, a reference to the vril in the midst of racist comments. Next slide please."

The references chosen to the subject of the subterranean worlds were numerous but not conclusive and the scholar was weaving with all of them a fabric that clearly showed that the Baron was avid to receive information coming from distant Tibet on the same subjects that the Nazis would collect eighteen years later.

"I could continue exhibiting daily quotes all morning, which would show that Ungern, so to speak, was gradually approaching the doors of Agartha." Said Eichenberg. "But I do not want to bore you with repetitive quotes, so let's move on to the most concrete and decisive paragraphs."

The scholar approached the site where Dennis was projecting the material and selected a group of slides at the end of the presentation.

" Show this one, please, it's dated at the beginning of 1921." He asked Dennis.

"Today I was visited by a traveler named Vitaly Kuznetsov, whom I was anxiously waiting for. According to the information I had received before, this man has been in one of the portals of Shambala or Agartha and explored hundreds of meters of very old carved galleries in all their length, with numerous engineering works to give stability to the construction. Hundreds of lateral branches were opened to the sides and the air circulated fluidly through holes strategically located in the roof of these caverns."

THE GOBI CODEX- LOST TREASURE BEYON A FLEEING HORIZON

" THIS TRAVELER WAS lead there by a monk disciple of the Panchen Lama, who is one of the greatest *connoisseurs* of the mysteries of Agartha, and who I suspect is either in telepathic contact with the inhabitants of the underground world, or directly is one of them. The portal is next to the river Sita, now called Tarim, which flows east from northern Tibet through Sinkiang. We have agreed with Kuznetsov that on his return from Russia we will both go to that site. The precise coordinates of this site are as follows." Then followed the precise geographic location of the portal, but had been crossed out both in the photo of von Ungern's diary and in the English translation, so that it was illegible.

A murmur ran through the meeting room. Dr. Richardson stirred in his chair and said.

"It is the first time we know of the existence of a concrete reference to the location of one of the entrances to the underground world. Dieter, do you have more material?"

"Yes, next slide, please."

" I just learned through a Mongolian rider that the Bolsheviks have captured Kuznetsov and sent him to a concentration camp in Siberia, I do not know if he is alive or dead, I will have to travel on the river Sita on my own."

"The last slide, please." Eichenberg asked Dennis.

"The Kingdom of Bogd Khan collapses, I will go out with my men to the Russian border tomorrow to try to contain them. The fortune-tellers predict that we will be defeated. We have agreed with the Khan that the royal treasury must be saved, as well as the official documentation of the kingdom, to preserve them from communist plunder and to have them available for a future restoration of the monarchy. I have selected my most loyal officers and the youngest soldiers to save this treasure from the clutches of the Bolsheviks. They will have the mission to travel all through the Gobi Desert to the north of Tibet, and guard the treasure inside the tunnels of Agartha whose portal we now know the location. May the gods bless that expedition so important for the future of Mongolia and our cause of restoration of the monarchy in these lands and in the motherland Russia."

"This is the last entry to Ungern's diary. As we all know, he was captured by the Bolsheviks and shot, so this message is his legacy." Said von Eichenberg.

He then sat down and was succeeded in speaking again by Jack.

"We can only partially reconstruct what happened next. The emissaries carrying the treasure and the documentation left for their destination on the Sita River, but for some reason they did not reach it. That is why they had to bury the treasure in the site of the Desert of Gobi to which the Russian clairvoyant Bodniev guided us. Later someone, knowing its location, took it out of its burial place in the desert and brought it to the cavern where we found it."

"Can this cavern be part of the subterranean world of Agartha?" Asked the lady who had made some comments previously.

Dr. Richardson got up elated from his chair and approached the woman whose hand he kissed.

"I'm introducing you to Madame Swarowska. Nadia is an old friend, she is a novelist of fertile imagination and I suspect she is also a seer, although she has always denied it." Addressing Jack and Dennis he added.

"Madame has asked a challenging question. Can you give an answer?"

Jack and Dennis were a bit bewildered. Finally Deborah, who had not spoken until then, said.

"Because we did not previously have all the information you just saw, we had not asked ourselves that question. We must recognize that it is pertinent because nobody knows what is the extension of the alleged underground kingdom so that we cannot exclude it a priori."

" In which case." Debbie continued. "The treasure bearers would have succeeded in placing it safely inside Agartha, although in fact they did not know it themselves because they were also unaware of everything we know today."

Encouraged by the good reception of her sister's speech, Selma overcame her shyness and said.

"It would even be possible that someone, knowing the secrets and extension of the system that we call today Agartha, has taken it from its original burial and has put it where we found it safe, then fulfilling in a deferred way the mandate of Baron von Ungern."

"Excellent observation! " Exclaimed obviously excited Richardson, as he realized the brainstorm that was being generated in the meeting, which marked the success of his management for having prepared it, which undoubtedly would have repercussions within the Bluthund Community. He continued.

" Any other comment or question?"

An elderly Japanese man who had remained silent until then raised a hand.

"Yes, Suzuki San." Richardson -who had taken over the role of master of ceremonies- granted the floor.

"I think that for today this is more than we can digest of a topic that most of us find totally new, even for me, that I am familiar with many Asian traditions."

The old man spoke with much aplomb and the others listened to him attentively, which evidenced its weight in the community. He continued.

"I propose that we approve everything that has been done and that we make a commission in our Community to analyze the issue in depth and make a recommendation on the steps to be taken from now on. The commission should make its decision shortly, for example within a period of fifteen days."

Richardson beat his palms excitedly.

"I support Suzuki San´s motion. Someone else?"

Madame Swarowska raised her hand in support.

"Well, we have a well-founded and duly supported motion. We will proceed to the voting in the usual way." Said Richardson, making a sign to the master of ceremonies. The man proceeded to circulate with a tray containing black and white ballots and an airtight container. Each member of Bluthund with the right to vote picked up one of the ballots and deposited it in the ballot box. Richardson was the last one. Then he and the master of ceremonies approached a small table and proceeded to recount the votes. Finally the latter moved to the center of the room, coughed to clarify his voice and attract the attention of the audience.

"The motion presented by the Honorable Suzuki San has been approved unanimously."

Chapter 21

When it was evident that the material earmarked to be exhibited was finished and the audience already showed a certain degree of fatigue, Dr. Richardson got up from his chair and walked up to the middle of the room. The man looked exultant.

" My dear friends, I believe that we have attended the exhibition of an important amount of unpublished material, which deals with a nebulous period of the history of Central Asia and that exposes some arcane of the oriental culture, which has always had fervent scholars in the West, both in their exo and esoteric shores. In accordance with the motion of Suzuki San approved by all, the actions of the members of the expedition have been approved by the Bluthund Community, on behalf of which we have the right to speak. It only remains to thank the aforementioned participants for their acceptance of the risks and hardships to which they were exposed, and those who were not already full members of our organization are received in their bosom with honors. This is the case of the Misses Deborah and Selma Liberman and the young Martín Colombo."

Then the master of ceremonies closed the meeting and invited attendees to a cocktail offered on the second floor of the building.

Deborah and Selma took a taxi to return home, since the latter had decided to spend the night at her sister's house and go to her parents the next day. Both were enthusiastic and remained silent for a while in the vehicle, while each processed the emotions originated by the event.

"Selma, you look beautiful." Finally said the elder. "You became the center of all men's looks and envy of all the women of the event."

As Selma remained silent, hiding her blush a bit, so her sister continued.

"In particular you had a devastating visual impact on Martín." Debbie exaggerated. "He did not open his mouth throughout the meeting and was following you with his eyes and almost jumped out of his chair when you spoke. And you did not direct him even one glance."

" That fool does not deserve it. He is probably enthralled with me now as he was in the desert with that Mongol girl."

"But I know that you like Martín from the moment you saw him for the first time. It does not make sense to hold resentments."

"Let him suffer as he has made me suffer before."

The aftermath of the meeting continued among the other attendees. Dennis and Martín also returned home together, although in the Subway. The young man looked absent and sad.

"The meeting was a total success and you have been admitted as a member of Bluthund, which is an honor reserved for few."

"I know that and I appreciate it".

Dennis looked at him straight and changed the subject.

"She looked beautiful, it was the feeling of all meeting attendants."

The young man blushed but persisted in his silence.

"Martín, what you feel is reciprocal, I assure you that the girl likes you."

" I do not know how you can say that. She despises me. She does not even look at me at all or speak one word to me."

"I do not think she despises you, although it may be that at this moment she hates you for reasons of jealousy. But that hatred hides another feeling."

"It hides it too well."

Dennis decided to leave the subject aside. He did not consider himself in a position to give sentimental advice and knew from experience that only time heals some wounds. To close the subject he then said.

"By your age it is expected that you do not understand women. I myself have difficulties sometimes to deal with them."

Not all the sequels of the Bluthund conclave were sentimental in nature. Once the guests had left and they found themselves alone in the spacious room, William Richardson invited Madame Nadia Swarowska and Taro Suzuki to have dinner in a small place adjoining the meeting room. The atmosphere was informal and relaxed, and the three had put aside a certain stiffness they had exhibited at the meeting. After a few moments the master of ceremonies joined, who also left out the subaltern treatment he had shown in the assembly.

"Sit down next to Nadia and serve yourself, we've already started." Said Richardson.

A few moments of silence marked the beginning of dinner until Suzuki literally exclaimed.

"Well, what a change of front this case had!"

"That's right." Richardson answered. "What had started as a kind of search for the plundered Mongolian treasure was transformed into something much more recondite with implications... I would call them, sinister."

" Were you aware of the links of Baron von Ungern with what happened later in Europe with the advent of Nazism?" asked Swarowska.

"Only through what characters such as protofascist Julius Evola and the creator of the Führerprizip, Hermann Keyserling wrote. "

"What do you think the alleged portal whose coordinates von Ungern gave can lead us to?" Richardson's question was addressed to the man who had acted earlier as the master of ceremonies.

"I rule entirely out that is something related to predecessors of the Aryan race or some other of the dreams of the Nazi occultists, but with something much more down to earth... more concrete." Said with security, while the other diners listened to him with attention.

" Do you think ..." Richardson began.

"It is not convenient to hypothesize yet. Instead I do think you have to alert our associates in London, Paris and Berlin, but do it with caution. Because of the nature of what may be at stake they have the right to know."

"You're right." Richardson affirmed. "I will speak with Sir David in London. You Nadia, can you do the same with our Paris associates?"

"And I'll talk to Berlin, where there can be more resentments." The master of ceremonies completed. "Taro, you can will obviously alert our friends in Tokyo."

There was consensus in the distribution of tasks. The host got up and said.

"I'll personally bring the dessert. Nadia, can you please take care of the coffee?"

When he was alone, Richardson looked dubiously at his watch. He wondered if it being ten o'clock in the evening in New York and taking into account the difference of time zones with the other side of the Atlantic his interlocutor would still be awake. Then he remembered the owl fame that the man had from his time of service in MI6, the mythical foreign intelligence service of the English government. Finally he decided to call, actually also to calm down his own anxiety.

An unmistakable voice answered the call on the fourth ring. Richardson could imagine his interlocutor in *robe de chambre*, slippers and reading a book near the fireplace.

"Sir David? I'm Richardson. If it's too late..."

"Ah! William. No, no. I was waiting for your call.

Sir David was aware that there was going to be a meeting in New York and its purpose. He had not been able to go because of his other commitments. Before the attentive silence of the other, Richardson told in detail what was done and said in the course of the event. When he considered that he had finished with the story he kept waiting for the questions that he knew would come. Sir David made a moment of silence, during which he was doubtless assessing what he had heard.

"THEN THE SUBJECT CAN go much further than the silly business of the Mongolian treasure." The phrase had the tone between an affirmation and a question.

"That's why I decided to call you at this time."

"I had heard before about that lunatic German or Russian and his Polish follower ... What was his name?"

" Ossendowski."

"Exactly, but I did not know that he had preceded the Nazis in their search for the origins of the Aryan race in Tibet."

Richardson dared to contradict the English but he did it with care.

"Sir David, according to rumors we received from other sources, it is not just that what can be hidden in those Godforsaken places."

"I'm listening to you, keep talking."

When the American finished with his explanation, Sir David exhaled a whistle.

"All right. There is no doubt that you must continue with your inquiry. Do you plan to organize another expedition?"

" Yes, in the next days."

" Do you currently have the coordinates of the site you are going to?"

"No, unfortunately the part of the diaries where they reproduced that data was erased in the presentation that was shown to us."

" Will you include the same participants in the expedition?"

"All those who live in New York. Five in total plus this specialist von Eichenberg."

"Okay, we have to limit the number of people who are aware of the purpose of this trip. Let me tell you two things."

They both made a few moments of silence while Sir David put his ideas in order.

" On the one hand I would like to have one of mine in your expedition. It is not a secret that there may be danger in it, and the person I would send, if you agree, is an expert in security, with let's say ... great skills."

"All right."

" Well, the code name of this person is Garland. This specialist will present to you in a few days, I ask you not to prejudge. It is one of my best assets...that is MI6's assets."

"All right."

"The second thing I wanted to tell you is something very unpleasant and I ask you to control your reactions."

"I hear you."

"We know that on the other side, you know what side I mean ... they have learned about the mission to the desert of Gobi and part of its results, although surely not of what you just told me because it is very recent."

Richardson felt as if a stone had fallen on his back.

"But ... that means ..."

"Actually, it means that there's a mole in Bluthund."

According to the established routine Gerda Schmiddel hit with her knuckles the heavy door a couple of times and entered. The Director was in front of his desktop computer on a small side table.

"Hans Wildau is entering the building." The woman had already passed a telephone call in which the aforementioned had requested an urgent interview with his superior.

"Thanks Gerda. Let him in as soon as he arrives."

The Director was intrigued by the urgency of his subordinate, always very unobtrusive and discreet. Once again the knocks sounded at the door and Wildau entered followed by the secretary.

" Shall I bring you some coffees?"

"Yes, please Gerda. Hello Hans, do sit down.".

The Director was perplexed. He had listened attentively to Wildau's long exposure and was now meditating on the possible implications of the news. At one point he decided that it was something he could not decide on his own, so he had to consult with his peers. He finally made a decision and said.

"Hans, can you wait for me here? I'm going to make a phone call."

Having said that, he got up and went to a small room next to the office, a place that was accessed only a few times in a month. There were an armchair and a small table with a telephone. It was a completely safe line. When the other side answered, the Director said.

THE GOBI CODEX- LOST TREASURE BEYON A FLEEING HORIZON

"OTTO? I'M HELMUT. I am calling you for something that has just been brought to my attention and may have unexpected derivations."

Then the Director repeated Wildau´s story. He ended by saying.

"I had heard of Ungern von Sternberg before and I knew he was one of our predecessors, but it never occurred to me that he could give actual clues about ... our goal."

On the other side the so-called Otto asked a question.

"Yes." answered the Director." The information comes from our usual sources in Bluthund. We totally trust him."

" Do not you know where they go to Tibet?"

"No, unfortunately the parts of von Ungern's diary where he gave the coordinates were masked in the slides and our contact did not have access to that information."

"We must prevent them from approaching our refuge. Try to divert those meddles from their route ... and if that fails do resort to other means. Can you trust Wildau for these tasks?"

"Totally. But I'll have to give him some reasons for our decisions."

" Do it, but only what is strictly indispensable for his mission. Only in a " need to know basis""

" Trust me."Suddenly exclaimed Helmut." Ah! There is another thing that worries me."

"Tell me about it."

"It is the presence in Bluthund's expedition of an offspring of one of the members of the Schäffer expedition."

" The one from 1938?"

"Yes."

"Keep me informed of that too."

Chapter 22

Preparations for the expedition began only the following week, with the aim of restoring traveler's energies and obtain the necessary visas and permits while assuring adequate financing. Dr. Richardson had put on his shoulders the burden to supervise every detail but the one who actually performed the actions was the master of ceremonies Watkins, a somewhat enigmatic character but who was undoubtedly the former's right hand.

The day before leaving, when both organizers were at the entrance of the building controlling the arrival of camping materials to the garage, a woman of small size separated from the rest of the by-passers and confronted them directly.

"Dr. William Richardson?"

"It's me."

"I'm Garland."

The aforesaid was stunned. His mind was busy receiving the material and being suddenly called by his name in the middle of busy Park Avenue was not part of his usual experiences. Also, although Sir David had warned him that he should not belittle the agent he was going to send him, Richardson really did not expect to meet a woman.

Maggie Garland, whether that was her real name or not, was a short woman with a slender body, dark hair in sharp contrast with her big blue eyes. It was difficult to calculate her age but Richardson estimated it between thirty and forty. Her face was pretty although it did not attract any attention; the man thought that this was appropriate for an agent of MI6, in short a spy, who had to merge with the rest of the people, to blend in with the environment.

Decidedly Richardson did not want to interview a secret agent on the street, so he left the supervisory functions in Watkins' hands. Then followed by the woman he entered the building, called the elevator and only when they were alone addressed her.

"You are welcome here. Excuse me for my initial reaction, but Sir David did not tell me that Garland was a lady."

" Does that bother you?"

"Not at all. He also told me that you are a very effective person in your work. How should I call you?"

" My colleagues usually call me Maggie."

When the presentations ended the woman said.

"I realize that you are very busy, so I do not want to steal your time. I need a place to work and have access to all the photographic and film material of the expedition to the Gobi Desert, and also personal information of the people who are going to accompany us. Excuse me but in my profession this is a fundamental requirement."

"I get it. Please follow me."

The man led his visitor into the great hall where the Bluthund assembly had taken place days before. He indicated the computer attached to the projector gun and located the relevant presentations in the PC hard disk. Then he excused himself, left the room for a moment and returned a few minutes later with some folders.

" I have files of the different members of the mission, but they do not know it and I would be in an embarrassing situation if they found out about their existence."

"Don't worry, in those who have my profession, discretion and secrecy are second nature."

"Can you manage alone with these equipment?"

"Of course."

THE GOBI CODEX- LOST TREASUREBEYON A FLEEING HORIZON

"I'll send my secretary with coffee and ask her to be at your service. She's totally trustworthy just like the man you met me down with, called Watkins."

Jerome Watkins was in charge of issues related to obtaining consular papers to travel to Tibet. This requires a Chinese visa and a special permit to visit Tibet, a region of the People's Republic of China. Travelers to Gobi already had a visa because they had been in Chinese territory and only had to get the special permit, the same as Garland, while von Eichenberg surprisingly had both.

Trips from J.F.Kennedy to Gonggar Airport in Lhasa would be made by Air China, and tickets would have an open return.

Obtaining permits to visit Tibet was facilitated by the fact that they were traveling as a group. The excuse provided was that of a trip of a religious nature and reservations were made to visit several monasteries and temples, including those of Sera and Jokhang in Lhasa as well as that of Pabangka, and also to the Potala Palace. Tourism in Tibet is massive, but close to 95% of the millions of travelers that arrive come from the rest of China. Much of Western tourism is related to the interest in Buddhism. Since he had good knowledge of the subject, von Eichenberg was in charge of giving all the answers to the consular questions.

The trip would include several hours spent in Beijing, but there would not be enough time to visit the Chinese capital, at least on the outward journey.

The expedition had been organized as a tourist excursion, the only way not to attract suspicion on the part of the Chinese authorities, always very prone to conceive doubts in everything related to Tibet. For this reason, visits to various temples and historical monuments, generally related to the Buddhist religion, had been interspersed, thinking that once they were made, the possible agents of the Chinese government would lose track of them.

Despite all this paranoid background, through their local contacts the Bluthund Community had managed to hire a Sherpa guide named Yeshe, who, according to Dr. Richardson explanations, had rendered different services before and was completely reliable.

Yeshe and two other Sherpas were waiting for the travelers in the esplanade of the hotel, in command of three utilitarian vehicles of Chinese origin that had a good load capacity and in spite of their rather unpromising aspect, were quite comfortable for the passengers. Jack and Dennis traveled with the guide; Deborah, Selma and Garland with one of the other two drivers and Martín and von Eichenberg with the third one.

According to plan during the first two days the travelers were on a trip of cultural and tourist purpose, which at the same time would give travelers the chance to socialize and get to know each other, particularly the two new members of the group, Garland and von Eichenberg.

Selma and her sister knew that their traveling companion was an agent of the English secret service, so their relationship was prudent at first, since they did not know what to expect from a woman with that job. However, once accustomed to the British accent of their companion the sisters found that it was a woman with the same interests as any other, and with a good deal of English humor. The driver, who did not speak a word of English, listened to the feminine talk like a mantra in the background sung by these strange priestesses.

Martín had high expectations for his trip with the expert in oriental philosophies and was glad when the man began to talk about trivial topics at the beginning of the journey that had the effect of breaking the ice. The young man was surprised when von Eichenberg started talking to the driver in what evidently was some Tibetan language. Then he remembered that the man already had not only a Chinese visa but also permission to travel through Tibet; for that reason he dared to ask.

" Mr. von Eichenberg, have you been to Tibet before?"

"Yes." Was the rather dry response that evidently showed he did not wish at that point to extend on the subject; however, immediately his expression softened and added.

"You can call me Dieter. Tell me, what have been your experiences during your stay in Mongolia?"

Martín evaluated with what degree of freedom to answer that question, but then reasoned that his partner was completely aware of the results of the previous expedition and began to narrate episodes that seemed to him outstanding of the aforementioned trip.

" How old are you, Martín?"

"Twenty-three years."

"And you have studies in your country?"

"I'm a recently graduated industrial engineer."

" Do you have experience in your profession?

"Not yet."

"But you have already had a number of adventures that few young people your age have experienced."

" Yes, I think that's the way it is."

"The professional expertise and everything else will come in due time, but the experiences you are having are irreplaceable and can only be acquired at your age."

The young man nodded again, attracted by the focus on which until that moment he had not had time to meditate.

The first two days went by as scheduled, and at the end of the second night, when they had set up their first open-air camp and had already eaten their early dinner, the guide Yeshe approached the fire around which the foreigners had gathered and participated in the talks. Finally he expressed.

" Tomorrow we leave the tourist side and we will go towards our goal."

" How far are we?"

" From now on we will leave the region of the lakes of high altitude and we will travel about 500 miles in southwest direction, towards the Himalaya mountains and Nepal. All of Tibet is at an average altitude of 4500 meters, but now we will go to the higher parts. Consider that these days have helped you to adapt your bodies to this altitude.

Chapter 23

According to what was anticipated by the guide, the road was effectively gaining altitude, which was perceptible in the foreigner's ears.

The distant line of summits became visible on the horizon first as a dark segment that with the passing of the hours began to emit flashes of bright white as they slowly approached the snowy peaks.

"Look at them from here." Yeshe said." You are contemplating the roof of the world."

Dennis, the navigator of the expedition, was permanently monitoring the course followed with his GPS, his compass and his maps, in which he was making notes for future reference. Both he and Jack were silent in order not to distract the driver's attention from his path, which was becoming intricate.

On the contrary, Martín talked animatedly with his new friend Dieter, who asked him questions about life in Argentina and at the same time satisfied the curiosity of the young man by telling him about his experiences in Tanzania.

In the other vehicle both Deborah and her sister had fallen asleep and Maggie Garland used that time to write a report on what happened in her slim notebook, thinking about transmitting it to her bosses when she arrived at a place that had internet and wi fi.

Gerda's voice rang on the intercom.

"*Herr Direktor*. You have a call from Hans Wildau from abroad."

"Please pass it on, Gerda."

There were some sounds and finally the familiar voice of Wildau sounded on the phone.

"Hello, Hans. What do you have for me?" Both interlocutors knew the advantages of making short calls in order to reduce the traceability by potential hostile elements, however small that possibility was.

"*Herr Direktor*. We have been able to find traces of an expedition that arrived four days ago in Lhasa. They are without a doubt the people we are looking for".

" Are you already in town?"

"Yes. I arrived last night".

The Director appreciated the effectiveness of his agent; he had just arrived a few hours before and yet he was after his prey.

"Well, will you go hunting?"

"As soon I can organize something. I reckon it will be tomorrow morning."

" Do you know our local contacts?"

"Not personally."

"I'll call them to make sure they give you all the necessary assistance."

"Thanks, *Herr Direktor.*

"Auf wiederhören.

"Auf wiederhören.

After ending the call with Wildau the Director meditated a few moments, extracted from one of the drawers of the desk an old black notebook from his laboratory times and called again Gerda Schmiddel.

"Gerda, please contact me with Colonel Liu Hung, in Beijing. Do you have the number?"

"Let me see ... I'm afraid not."

"Look under Hung Liu. The first name is Hung."

"Let's see ... yes, here I have it. I will communicate you with him right away."

The ascending path had taken them to the first foothills of the Himalayas. The air had become poorer in oxygen, so that at each altitude increase their metabolisms had to get regularized to avoid fatigue. All day long they were driving through paths progressively narrower and steeper. The villages and the flocks became increasingly scarce, spaced and small, until finally they only occasionally saw a shepherd looking for a lost sheep or a solitary lama on his pilgrimage to his cubicle located in some hidden cave. Every so often the passengers rotated between the three vans, in order to refresh the conversations that were exhausted during the monotonous trip. At least, Nature constantly gave them renewed landscapes and new emotions in the form of narrow cornice paths stretching on slopes bordering unfathomable precipices. Selma tried to overcome her natural propensity to vertigo but still closed her eyes when going through a particularly distressing narrowness. Her sister did not separate from her side and Dennis had joined in the vehicle and with his serene prose sought to reassure the women.

Martín had boarded the truck that was carrying Jack, a character that had dazzled him for his true narrations of episodes lived in different continents and natural environments. The young man's insatiable thirst for adventure was aroused by Berglund's austere stories, and he constantly asked for extensions of details about characters, circumstances, times and places, which his interlocutor could sometimes only satisfy half-heartedly, since these were confidential missions that Bluthund had confided to him.

Garland had replaced Martín as a companion of von Eichenberg and although at first she had to overcome a certain reluctance that the English have towards the Germans, she soon began to feel comfortable with the plain personality of the man, who also asked her to call him by his first name. Due to her profession and unlike Martín, what interested the woman were not colorful stories from previous experiences but hard data that could be stored on her mind hard drive and that would allow Garland to complete a mental dossier and compose a character. To carry out this task Garland used the soft and non-invasive interrogation techniques in which the English police stand out. As the talk time passed, the woman felt a dangerous sense of attraction with which she wanted to litigate to avoid clouding her judgment.

"But you're not pure German, your features are clearly mixed."

"That's right."

"Don't you want to elaborate a little more your answer?"

"My paternal grandfather married a Tibetan woman."

"Surprising. What led a German aristocrat of the Nazi period to marry a non-Aryan woman?"

"Love, I suppose."

"Who was she? The daughter of some diplomat or member of the ruling castes of Tibet, who at that time were allies of Japan?"

Dieter thought for a moment and responded with aplomb.

" Nothing of that. She was a priestess and a Tibetan ritual dancer. My ancestor met her in a monastery, where he was being instructed by an old lama in the Tibetan variant of Buddhism."

"A variant of Tantrism?"

"Yes."

" What was your Tibetan grandmother's name?" "Tara."

"And has something from her cultural legacy reached you?"

"A lot."

"And does it make you proud?"

"Yes." The man's responses tended to become monosyllabic. Garland felt that the attraction for the character that was building inside her increased and realized that at some point she would not manage that impulse and feared that the control she wanted to impose on her own feelings was at risk.

"Tell me about your grandfather."

"What do you want me to say?"

"Let's start by his name."

"Wolfram. His name was Wolfram.

"And what was Wolfram doing in Tibet at that time?"

Dieter was actually waiting for the woman's direct question and decided to open up.

"He was part of a German expedition in Tibet."

" That of Ernst Schäffer in 1938?"

The fact that the Englishwoman was aware of this activity lost in the dust of History surprised Dieter.

"Yes."

" So Grandpa Wolfram was looking for the ancestors of the Aryan race in this part of Asia?" The tone of the question was a bit sarcastic, and as she noticed it the woman excused herself. "Excuse me, I did not mean to be rude."

"The question is valid. But the grandfather was not a Nazi. He was young man who, precisely because of his aristocratic background, did not believe in these hoaxes. That put him at risk because in the group there were members of the SS, whose chief Himmler was one of the sponsors of the expedition."

"So grandfather Wolfram must have kept his aristocratic opinions to himself."

"Not with too much success apparently."

"What do you mean?"

"Apparently Wolfram deserted and was chased by his comrades. The monastery -led by his tutor the lama who led Wolfram in his Buddhist instruction- gave him and Tara protection in a mountain refuge. They remained there for five years, the entire period of the Second World War. My father and his three brothers were born there. My grandfather only returned to Germany with his wife and children in 1955."

Maggie Garland remained silent for a few seconds; then she asked with complete candor.

"You are here with us in search of your roots. Is that true?"

This time Dieter did not expect that disturbing question since even he had not considered his own reasons so crudely.

"I imagine it's like that, as you say."

For a few moments they remained silent, assimilating the effects of the talk in each one. Suddenly the man asked.

" I feel that I have been subjected to an interrogation, soft and cordial but exhaustive, by someone who is trained in these techniques."

A brief pause followed, then the German continued with the same brutal frankness.

"Who are you? What is your role in this expedition?"

This time the one who had not seen the question coming was Maggie, so she tried to divert it.

"What do you mean?"

"You know perfectly what I want to say."

The woman felt herself cornered, and began to regret having started the investigation. But immediately she overcame the embarrassment and answered with confidence.

"I'm here to take care of the security of this expedition and its members."

"But you are not a member of this brotherhood, I mean the Bluthund Community. It is not true?"

"No, I'm not. But I beg you not to ask any more questions at this time."

"All right."

Garland wrapped herself in a blanket she had carried on his trip in anticipation of the low temperatures. The woman closed her eyes and fell asleep with an unexpected sweet taste in his mouth.

Hans Wildau was sitting in an armchair in the lobby of the hotel in Lhasa. The director had personally called him the night before to let him know that the arrangements for the trip were made and that someone would be meeting him in the hotel in the morning. The expedition leader would identify himself with the Jade Black password.

He was already half asleep after a couple of hours of waiting when a sixth sense warned him that he was in someone's presence. Startled he opened his eyes and found that a young Chinese woman dressed in a grim manner was watching him about four paces away. Quite disoriented, Wildau jumped up.

"I'm Black Jade." said at once the woman in English.

The man's confusion increased and he could not hide it. He had expected the contact to be a German resident in Tibet, and logically he expected a man.

"I'm not what you expected. Is not true?"

"No ... I ... I'm sorry, I was asleep."

"Do you have your luggage ready?" Asked the woman without concessions. Wildau wondered if a smile had ever appeared on that beautiful oriental face.

"Yes, it's in that corner." He said pointing to a place out of the way of the many tourists passing by. "And I've already paid the hotel bill."

He extended his right hand and the woman shook it tightly.

"Hans Wildau."

" Liu Daiyu. Or if you prefer. Daiyu Liu."
" Your given name is ... Daiyu?"
"Yes."
"It has any meaning? Chinese names usually have poetic meanings."
"It means precisely Black Jade." The woman answered dryly.

Suddenly Wildau was invaded by the feeling that the young woman's harsh look and treatment was a mask that protected an interior that she feared would be exposed. He decided not to be impressed or driven by those external signs and to respond with cordiality to start dissolving that shell. He was aware that the woman attracted him strongly.

The convoy of three vehicles had crossed a zone of continuous and steep ascent arriving finally at a flat plateau of several hectares of surface, surrounded by high peaks. Jack and Dennis talked with the Tibetan guide and both men agreed to spend the night in that place. The tents were placed and two fires were lit, one for Tibetan drivers and one for travelers. Dennis and Deborah were in charge of preparing the food and Selma and Martín cleaned afterwards the used elements and buried the waste. They sat next to the fire that burned brightly despite the shortage of oxygen in the air. Dieter had walked about thirty or forty paces away, near the edge of the plateau and was looking at the sky. Garland called him and the man turned and with a broad gesture pointed to the sky and the abyss before him. Intrigued the Englishwoman stood up and approached. When she stood next to the man and contemplated the firmament could not contain a soft exhalation. Far from the glow of the fire and in the absence of moonlight myriads of stars shone around, up and sideways until their light was intercepted by the dark masses of the surrounding mountains. Nature offered all its splendor at that point close to the roof of the world. Maggie felt her chest fill with air and her retinas filled with star light. Without saying a word, Dieter took the left hand of the woman with his right hand and both remained silent and silent, in order not to break the magnetism of the situation.

Far away from there, by the campfire Deborah looked at the couple and then alternately at Dennis, who was watching her with a smile. From the bonfire around which the Tibetan guides were sitting, a strange melody of the three voices was accompanied by a curious string instrument. The music did not seem to have articulated lyrics but a series of sounds that at first seemed monotonous. Suddenly Selma began to hum along the melody and soon everyone was singing the son.

The magic of the moment and place lasted for a while and was recorded in the unconscious of each of those present. The music of the Tibetans finally became extinct and the couple left the edge of the abyss and rejoined each other's place next to the fire, whose psychological function was to keep away the threats of the monsters of darkness that are lodged in the collective unconscious of the humans.

Deborah was preparing to go to her tent to sleep when she looked at her sister. The girl was tense, her eyes closed and a slight tremor shook her body. Alarmed Debbie came over and touched her on the shoulder. The girl opened her eyes staring straight ahead.

"Selma. What's wrong with you? " Said the worried sister as all eyes converged on them. At first it seemed that the girl had difficulty speaking but after a few seconds she said.

"Someone observes us. Someone is watching us from the dark or at least intends to do it."

Chapter 24

The expedition members looked at each other. Maggie Garland had a skeptical look at what she thought was a paranoid access, but Jack, who guessed her thoughts, warned her.

"Selma does not suffer from delusions but has powers of clairvoyance. We have had plenty of chances to check them in the near past."

Dennis stood up, took an iron in his hands and said softly.

"I'm going to walk around. Jack, stay here to take care of the camp.

"I'm going with you." Garland's voice rang unexpectedly and Dieter tried to stop it.

"Let me do it, I'll go with Dennis."

Without answering a word the English pulled out an unsuspected gun from one of the pockets of her trousers and approached the man who was already leaving. Both carried lanterns to guide themselves in the thick darkness.

THE GOBI CODEX- LOST TREASURE BEYON A FLEEING HORIZON

Time passed slowly for the travelers sitting around the fire. Deborah was holding on her lap the head of her sister, who after the vision had deeply fallen asleep perhaps due to the effort of concentration made. Martín looked at both women with a thousand fantasies circulating in his mind while Jack walked every so often around the perimeter of the camp, monitored by one of the Tibetan guides who took turns sleeping.

<We have an organized camp.> The man thought, without falling into a self-complacency that could be dangerous.

Two interminable hours later Maggie Garland and Dennis returned.

"Nothing, we have not seen anything." The man informed.

"Anyway, we're going to organize three-hour watches to make sure there's no danger around." added. the Englishwoman. "We cannot ignore any sign."

Dennis had told her in their long exploration of Selma's previous intuitions and their results, to which the travelers in the Gobi Desert undoubtedly owed their lives.

Martín was struggling with drowsiness to finish his duty shift, for which there was still a half hour to go that seemed a very long time. He added a couple of dry wood branches to the embers and in the light of the renewed fire he saw a shadow carefully approaching Garland's tent. When he recognized the figure of Dieter von Eichenberg he smiled. The man disappeared inside the tent.

Wildau tried to fit inside the Chinese truck, which did not have a good suspension among its virtues. In front of him sat the hieratic Liu Daiyu looking straight forward. In the same vehicle were two other armed men, with the same immovable position of the woman. In each of the other two trucks, six more men traveled. The German had enough experience to recognize military behavior in any country in the world. He had already drawn his conclusions and had no doubts about them. Those were soldiers of the Chinese Army and Black Jade was their leader, of whose minimal gestures all the men were attentive.

They had already traveled for an hour and Wildau decided to speak to Daiyu suddenly so as to find her with low defenses. Following a hunch, he did it in German.

"Black Jade. What rank have you?"

The woman reacted with a start and answered in the same language.

"What do you mean?"

"I asked what your military rank is."

" To what rank are you referring?"

"You know it well. To your rank in the Chinese People's Army."

Seeing that any denial would be useless, the woman regained her composure and answered with the characteristic succinctness.

"Captain. I am an infantry captain."

"And the older man who travels in the back vehicle is your sergeant?"

"Yes, he's Sergeant Cheng."

For the first time Daiyu looked straight at Wildau and her eyesight was lost in his blue eyes, which was exactly what he wanted to promote from the beginning. The German observed the perfect oval of the girl's face and her delicate features. He regretted that the heavy uniform did not allow him to appreciate her curves. Neither her clothing, nor that of her men, nor the vehicles wore insignias that would allow an observer to identify them as military.

" The weapons that you carry belong to the Chinese army?"

"No.".

"What are they, AK47 of Russian origin?"

"Mostly yes."

" So that there is nothing that relates you to the army nor the Chinese government?"

"Nothing." In spite of herself Daiyu had to admire the clear mind of the man who was in front of her. Precisely the trait that most admired the girl in a man was intelligence. Stimulated by the ice break the girl wanted to evacuate some doubts so she asked several questions, although she could not prevent blushing when doing so.

" Your name is Hans, right?"

"Yes."

" Have you had military training?

"Didn´t your bosses give you a dossier with my data?"

" Yes, but that info was not there."

"Not military, but in the secret services of what was then my country."

"What country was that?"

"The German Democratic Republic."

"That is to say communist Germany?"

"Yes."

"So you are, or rather you were, an intelligence agent, a spy."

"Right."

Then the girl confided that she wanted to specialize in intelligence in the Chinese army. The conversation became fluid and the German changed his place, sitting next to the woman. A quick check of the other soldiers allowed him to see that they were still staring straight ahead, whatever was going through their minds when they saw his movement. As he approached her he could feel a mild fragrance emanating from Daiyu's hair.

"Do you have any clue where we should go?" He asked the girl.

"We are looking for them by air and by land."

Wildau was surprised to learn the means that had been mobilized for the task. He asked himself what would be the contacts of the Director in the Chinese government and what could be the motive that would guide them. He approached his face to the girl's face and whispered in her ear.

"I like your aroma."

The next day passed on an uneven terrain and the rattle of the vans was incessant. Dieter tried to concentrate on the detailed reading of the photos of the pages of Baron Ungern's diary but it was a difficult task even for the methodical German scholar.

"It's like trying to read inside a washing machine." He exaggerated but continued with his efforts.

After two and a half an hour they stopped for lunch. The travelers left the vehicles to prepare the food and stretch their legs. Deborah asked Maggie Garland.

"I have not seen Dieter. Do you know where he is?"

"Dieter was in that vehicle. He is struggling with those photos of the von Ungern diary he has in his notebook. I'm going to tell him to join us taking advantage of the detention time."

When she returned to the vehicle the Englishwoman found Eichenberg holding the computer on his knees and looking forward with a lost look.

"What happens, Dieter?"

The man suddenly returned to reality and answered.

" I found a clue we had missed before."

"What is it about?"

"One mention of another entrance to the tunnel system, that is, another portal of the alleged underground city."

"How is it that nobody had seen it before, neither you nor the others who analyzed the material?"

" Ungern himself has underestimated it. It seems that he did not give much credit to the gossip of the lamas who had provided the data."

" Do you have the coordinates?"

"Yes, as a good soldier Ungern had taken the trouble to locate the site even though he did not believe in its existence."

"I'm going to call Dennis to ascertain the location of that place."

They had cleared a section of the stone floor in order to display a large map. Dennis was with the GPS in his hand and finally said while pointing to a spot on the paper.

"It's about this place." It's quite close, beyond those low hills."

" What importance do you attribute to this new data?"" Asked Jack who had just arrived.

"I do not know."

"I think that being so close we cannot just pass by." added realistically Dennis. "We must go and visit it. It is the first track that is presented to us."

"All right. As soon as we finish lunch some of us will approach that spot in one of the vehicles. The rest will remain here. The guide, Dennis, Dieter and I will go." concluded Jack.

"I must be included in the group. There might be security hazards in that trip." The voice of Maggie that had approached and heard the last sentences was heard. "There's room enough in the van for all."

The vehicle reached a point where the path that lay ahead was blurred and finally ended in a scree. The four travelers got out of the car and tried to orient themselves.

"We are practically in the place." said Dennis. "We must look for an entrance to a grotto or cavern or something similar. Doesn't the diary give any clues?"

"We must remember that von Ungern himself was never here. Let me see once more the text that mentions the site."

Then he turned on the notebook again and reviewed the mention of the portal. After a few moments he exclaimed.

"It says the portal is at the foot of a "chess horse."

" Chess horse! What the hell is that?"

"I cannot know. Let's look around to see if we can find something that can be assimilated to that strange description."

Everyone began to walk around in the unlikely search. The vehicle guide got out of it and asked Dieter if he could help. The offer was immediately accepted since an extra pair of eyes increased the chances of achieving some result.

After a while Maggie exhausted by fatigue had sat on a rock. She covered her eyes with her hat to avoid the glare of the sun. After a few moments she turned around herself and discovered her face. Once her eyes adjusted to the light again, she frowned and asked in a low voice.

" What is that, at the top of that hill?"

"What do you mean?" Asked Dieter, who had managed to hear her voice.

In response, the woman pointed to a strange formation on the summit of an elevation about three hundred paces.

"Do you think it has the shape of a horse's head?" The German asked.

"No, but it's strange."

" Do not forget that Ungern had only reproduced the comments of a Tibetan lama. We have to look at that mound with Tibetan eyes." He immediately called the guide and asked him in his language. Maggie was surprised when the man answered aloud while nodding ostensibly. The girl then looked at Dieter and saw that he exhibited a smile. She ask.

"All right. What has the guide said?"

"Well, he says that he sees it as a horse's head although he personally does not know what chess is."

In the absence of better tracks the four travelers met and decided to go up to the elevation and search the site.

"In the worst case from there we will have a better view of the surroundings." Jack consoled himself.

The ascent was slow, since the slope was quite large and they had to overcome all kinds of rocky obstacles so that the path was zigzagging. Dieter had to lean heavily on a rock and asked the woman.

" How come you are in such physical good condition?"

"I practice aerobics three times a week."

"Always?"

"Always."

Somewhat embarrassed, the man shook his head and went on painfully.

Finally the guide arrived at the summit and once there he waited for the remaining mountaineers to meet him. Meanwhile, the Tibetan looked around the ground and the slope. When Dennis and Maggie arrived he pointed to a hole in the base of the alleged horse's head making comments with big gestures.

"What does he say?"

"That there may be an entrance there." replied Dieter, who was finally arriving

Again the travelers sat on the ground to take a breath as the altitude limited their supply of oxygen; the woman was the first to stand up and to incite the men who were ashamed to follow her. Preceded by the guide they approached the rugged crevice feeling immediately the freshness of its internal medium after the prolonged exposure to the dehydration in full sunlight as they climbed the hillside. On the other hand, what could be seen of the interior was not very promising, with ridges with serrated edges up to where the light reached.

"All right. What do are we waiting for? Who goes to the front? " Continued hurrying the woman, until with a resignation gesture Dieter entered the crack.

Chapter 25

After a short walk from the entrance of the cavern, the light from the outside was extinguished and only the thin luminous fingers of the hand torches remained. Those who had been on the expedition in the Gobi Desert were soon able to compare this cave with the one they had found then. In the new case the corridor was always narrow, twisted in such a way that the travelers felt as if they were turning 180 degrees and approaching in a circular way the slope they had entered. The ground was strewn with debris and the roof had dangerous points that had to be avoided to prevent having the skull torn by the protrusions. At least in the new cave there were no lateral branches that made travelers fear losing their way in the belly of the mountain. The direction of the march was clearly descending, which could not be otherwise given that they had entered at the very top of the mountain.

Insensibly the width of the passageway started widening and the space with the irregular roof extended, which gave a little more comfort to the displacements of the explorers. The Tibetan guide had a fearful gesture on his face, no doubt for superstitious reasons, so that finally Dieter authorized him to return to the surface and wait there. Although he did not want to acknowledge himself, his decision was also influenced by the desire to keep confidential the possible findings that could be made in the cave, which would become doubtful having within the group persons moved by other purposes than those of the Bluthund Community.

The minutes passed quickly and finally totaled an hour of exploration. Jack was worried about the possible difficulties that could be found when retracing their steps, but in a second analysis he thought that since there were no branches in the tunnel they could not get lost in the heart of the mountain.

"Do not you notice?" Maggie said unexpectedly. "The air is getting thicker."

"It is natural because we are moving more and more away from the entrance, and there does not seem to be another air inlet." answered the German.

The passageway ahead of them traced the umpteenth curve so that they prepared to take it by going in single file because in those cases the tunnel narrowed. Dennis went to the front and illuminated the space before him with the narrow beam of light from the lantern. After a prolonged silence he suddenly exhaled an obscenity.

"What's wrong?" asked alarmed Maggie Garland.

"The tunnel ends suddenly ... right here."

The four walkers turned speleologists entered a short cavity that was on the other side of the curve and found that, indeed, that was the end of the road. A sense of frustration invaded the explorers by the abrupt end of a quest that looked promising when they had entered the cave.

"Let´s not get discouraged." Said Dennis."Don't forget that the location we are after is the one Baron Ungern had marked in his diary as the main one, and this was a secondary possibility of which until a few hours ago we had no knowledge."

"He's right, let's not be overcome by frustration." Jack completed, sitting on the rocky ground. "Let's rest for a while before starting the way back."

The others imitated his action since the oxygen shortage in the inner air of the cave diminished their energies. Jack closed his eyes, Dennis leaned his back against the rock wall and rested his neck on it, Dieter placed his head on his knees and stood still in that position, while Maggie took off her boots and rubbed her feet. When she picked up one of the shoes from the ground to put it back on a strange object shone in the light of the torch resting on the ground.

"What is this? It looks like a metallic object." said the woman, as she picked it up and shook the dust that covered it." It's like a coin."

Tediously everyone overcame their drowsiness and directed their respective lights towards Maggie´s hand . Suddenly old family stories flashed back in Dieter´s mind, which in a somewhat impolite gesture pounced on the site of the find and removed the object from the woman's hand. For a moment he lacked breath.

"YES ... IT'S JUST AS my grandfather described it to me. Oh Maggie! Excuse me for my manners." As he said this he delicately passed a handkerchief across the surface of the object and exclaimed." There it is!"

" What grandpa are you talking about? And what the hell have you found? " asked Jack somewhat perplexed.

"I will explain that later. Let's look if we find something else."

"Something like what?"

"Other coins or bone remains."

In the dim light of the lanterns whose batteries were already extinguishing all began to nervously dig the rock floor covered with the dust of the centuries, until Dennis exclaimed.

"Yes. Here is something ... it can be a piece of bone, although a bit strange."

The search was continued until all the substrate covering the floor of the cavity was removed without further findings.

"This gives me a deep emotion." Dieter looked really shocked.

"Why? How did you know there could be bones?" Jack was puzzled.

" It's amazing ... my grandfather was in this same place in 1938." Dieter seemed delirious. "The chances of me returning to the same place two generations later were tiny, and yet it happened."

While Jack looked dumbfounded, a certain explanation began to form in Maggie's mind based on isolated things the German had told her. Meanwhile, Dennis, always practical, was exploring the walls of the redoubt they were in.

" This tunnel originally continued further, this obstacle that is in front of us is just a wall of rubble, product of a landslide."

Resigned to not being able to understand Dieter's babbling, Jack sat up and joined Dennis.

" You are right, these are rocks that at some point in its history have fallen in some catastrophe inside the cavern. It is possible that the tunnel went further."

Dieter who seemed recovered from his shock joined the conversation, which brought some relief to Maggie.

"It is important that we record these findings adequately for further research. Although it is doubtful that anyone comes this way, the place where we find these remains must be well documented. When we leave the cave I will try to explain what happens, at least as far as I know."

The others retreated behind the curve to leave the collapsed room empty, while Dennis filmed and photographed the site, including the objects found, which for that purpose had been placed back where they had been found. The man was at the same time recording an accurate description of what was done.

Finally everyone loaded their equipment and started back, but thanks to Maggie's chance finding the previous depressing atmosphere had been replaced by a festive mood.

THE GOBI CODEX- LOST TREASURE BEYON A FLEEING HORIZON

That night the group returned late to the camp and found that the two guides who had remained in the camp had already dined so that they prepared to eat alone. Deborah, Selma and Martín were somewhat concerned about their delay but the Englishwoman gave an explanation of circumstances about what happened on the ride.

"I hope that later Dieter will be able to make some sense in what we have found."

The German joined the rest when they had eaten, his face looked radiant despite his two days beard and obvious fatigue and dined hastily while the others were waiting for him. Finally Jack spoke on behalf of everyone.

"Can you tell us what happened in that cave and what did we find?"

Dieter had come with a backpack from which he removed some plastic envelopes where he had placed the objects they had found, after proceeding to their careful cleaning, following the usual protocols in the archaeological excavations. He passed the artifacts to Maggie who was placed on his right asking her that after watching them to pass to the rest of the members of the expedition. Meanwhile he started with an explanation with his German accent.

"In 1938, my grandfather Wolfram von Eichenberg was in this same place with an expedition organized by the Thule Society, an organization that had developed certain theories that the SS chiefs would later make their own."

" So your grandfather was a Nazi."

"In fact he wasn't. That's why he had to hide in Tibet."

While Maggie heard Dieter repeating that part of the explanation that she already knew, her brain disciplined by the English secret services connected some dots and extracted certain conclusions based on previous suspicions. Finally the woman drew an action plan in her mind, and wondered how to communicate it to her fellow adventurers.

Chapter 26

" So this swastika that we see in the medal or coin was not carved by the Nazis?" asked Martín.

"NO. IT IS A VERY OLD object, whose age is measured in thousands of years and perhaps tens of thousands. That swastika, turning in the

same direction as that of the Nazis or in the opposite direction, is found in carvings on rocks in various parts of Asia and although some attribute it to the emergence of Indo-Europeans or Aryans in these latitudes, even that is not sure." Dieter paused.

"The really amazing thing is to have found it -as my grandfather did in the last century- in the context of a cave with skeletal remains that are not fully human. Although they are hominids, as you can see the thickness of the cranial bone is excessive to be of one member of our *homo sapiens* species."

"What explanation do you have for those bones?" asked Debbie. " Did they belong to the proto-Aryans the Nazis were looking for?"

"The truth is that I do not have an explanation. This is the beginning of an investigation and not the end."

" And you say that your grandfather had found the same objects?"

" Yes, although the piece of skull was of a different bone, so that it is possible that both came from the same skull."

" And what repercussion had your Grandpa's finding?" Now who asked was Jack.

"I do not know because the whole discussion took place in a Nazi milieu that Wolfram was excluded from. In any case, do not forget that this happened in 1938. The following year the Second World War broke out and the interest and resources were transferred to the actions of war."

"Don´t you know if the allies, particularly the English, learned of this finding at the end of the war?" Maggie's question seemed a little out of place to the others.

"I do not know exactly. What I remember of the family narratives is that when Wolfram returned to Germany in 1954 the English were in Berlin at the time and he was interrogated by MI6."

Upon hearing this response Maggie had an imperceptible shock.

The next day, before leaving for the new destination at the coordinates indicated by von Ungern, Jack decided to make a call via the satellite phone to Dr. Richardson. Maggie approached him hesitantly.

" Are you going to call your boss?"

"Yes."

" Can you lend me the phone later? I would also like to call mine."

"No problem."

The woman seemed hesitant.

"Hey Jack, can I propose something to you?"

"What is it about?"

"Can we coordinate what we are going to say."

The man seemed somewhat hesitant, but replied.

"I'm listening..."

When trying to start the three vehicles one of them refused to work. Two of the drivers got under the hood of the truck to check the engine, particularly the ignition system. Finally Dennis joined them but the solution did not appear until late afternoon, so they decided to postpone the departure for the next day, in order to make the whole journey in daylight and in a single stage.

That night Wildau slipped into Daiyu's tent, not paying much attention to the sentry stationed in the camp, who kept his eyes fixed on the horizon and pretended not to see anything.

THE GOBI CODEX- LOST TREASURE BEYON A FLEEING HORIZON

AT ONE POINT THE MAN'S phone rang and he proceeded to answer the call immediately.

"*Ja, Herr Direktor*. As he remembered that the woman understood some German and preferred to keep discretion in the conversation, Wildau left the tent and was talking outside for several minutes. Finally he ended the call and re-entered the tent.

" Was your boss?"

"Yes."

"And have you any news?"

The man's face lit up in one of his rare smiles.

"Yes."

"You look happy. They must be good. Share them with me"

"The coordinates of the place of the discovery are being sent to me. Your people will make an aerial reconnaissance of the place."

"Good." Daiyu said in a feline tone." Now come with me."

"How about that?" Hans asked sarcastically. "What has become of the typical oriental woman, discreet and demure?"

"You're not talking to a housewife but to a captain of the Chinese People's Army, remember?"

AT DAWN THE NEXT DAY Selma woke up startled and sat in her sleeping bag. Debbie, who had already gotten up and was folding her own sleeping bag, asked, surprised.

"Selma, dear. Is something happening to you?"

"They are looking for us."

"Who are looking for us and where?"

"I do not know who they are, but they are close."

Both women left the tent to allow Martín to disassemble it and approached Maggie, Dieter and Jack, who were having breakfast.

" Tell them about your premonition." Debbie urged her sister.

"I woke up with the certainty that someone is looking for us and that is near here."

The three interlocutors looked at each other in a meaningful way.

"What else can you tell us?"

"I do not know what they are looking for but their intentions are not good."

Seeking to soothe her, Jack stroked the head of the girl who looked frightened.

"All right. Go to get breakfast and let us take care of it."

The young girl left but her sister stayed with the group.

"Why do I have the feeling that you are not only not surprised but that you were kind of expecting it?"

"We were not waiting for it for sure, but it was one of the possibilities ... of the worrying possibilities." Jack answered enigmatically, showing signs of not wanting to elaborate on his answer.

With her usual agility, the result of exercise and her light body, Maggie climbed a hill that even though it was not too high, allowed her to look at the horizon in almost all directions. She pulled down the brim of her Australian hat to keep the sun from dazzling her and took the binoculars from its case, sweeping the sky in all directions.

When she saw it, the woman made a slight sound. It was like a little insect fluttering over the peaks at a certain distance. At that moment Dieter approached and the woman handed him the binoculars pointing in a certain direction.

" It's a helicopter. They fly low and in circles. No doubt they are looking for something on the ground."

Just then, Jack joined in, and heard the last sentence. Dieter handed him the binoculars.

"They are looking for us." concluded Jack""Once again Selma was right."

"Shall we hide the vehicles and the camp?" asked Dieter.

"We will not hide, they would detect us anyway."

The buzzing of the aircraft came to them. The size of it enlarged in the sunlight and soon a flash wounded the retina of the travelers.

"They've seen us." Maggie said. "They just do not know we've seen them too."

At that moment the helicopter spun around and away from the site at full speed.

"They are there." Daiyu said in a low voice as she cut off her communication. "We will get moving right now. They are not far. We will arrive at dawn."

"It may be that they have left the spot by then." Argued Wildau.

"Does not matter. We already have the coordinates of the place. If we also want the travelers we can always detect them from the air again."

She immediately left her tent and began to give orders to her men, who immediately set to work. Wildau watched admiringly from the tent door the feverish activity that the woman had unleashed.

"We'll start moving towards our target at dawn. "Said Jack, who somehow and by consensus of the group acted as a virtual leader. "We should reach our goal soon after noon."

And in this way, all the players of this complex plot advanced towards its final phase, heading to a conflict that looked inevitable and whose outcome was not yet written. Behind each of those characters there were puppeteers who pulled their strings to achieve their own purposes.

"They have already set off for the final stage." William Richardson said to his silent interlocutor.

"All according to plan?"

"Yes."

" When are they planning to arrive?"

"In the course of the afternoon."

"Let me know as soon as you have news."

"Of course. Sir David. Count on that."

The journey took longer than expected due to the route full of obstacles and the narrow and dangerous trails, In fact it was already four in the afternoon and the travelers had not yet reached the coordinates sought. Selma had insisted on traveling in the first vehicle along with Jack and Dennis, who officiated as a navigator.

"The succession of peaks makes the distances on the map misleading."

"In addition all these curves and counter-curves tend to disorient the most experienced traveler." Answered the former. " It forces me to be constantly consulting the compass."

"But surely we are on the right path."

The girl traveled in silence and at times closed her eyes as if she were asleep. At one point she asked the men to stop the vehicle. Although he was a bit surprised Jack ordered the driver to stop at a small landing, while indicating the remaining vehicles to do the same by waving his arm up and down.

While the group members stretched their legs Selma climbed a steep rock that nevertheless offered a practicable path to the top. Martín decided to follow her to make sure she did not suffer a setback that could be risky. The young woman came up with unexpected agility and forming a screen over her eyes with her left hand began to look at the horizon.

Deborah and Dennis were talking about the exceptionally mild climate they were enjoying at that time of the year and soon Maggie joined them in order to participate in some banal conversation after the silent trip.

"Although I suffer the cold weather until now I cannot complain..."

Her words were interrupted by a scream that came from above. The unmistakable voice of Selma was repeated by the echo of the mountains. When they looked at her, they saw her pointing to a place in the sky.

"There it is ... it's that ... the star of Agartha."

It was almost seven o'clock when they arrived at the place indicated by the GPS. A mass of dark rock rose in front of them and in all likelihood that was the site they were seeking and all they could do at that time was to determine if there was an entrance to a cave as expected based on previous experiences.

"To continue in the midst of this darkness is dangerous. We will make a camp here, so we can restore our strength and tomorrow at dawn we will go to the search. " Expressed Jack before the consensus of the others.

After dinner Debbie and Dennis went for a walk on the wide plateau that opened before them. They stood in front of a precipice beyond which and at a great distance, snowy peaks extended. The silence was only broken by the soft whistle of a breeze and both watched the sunset behind the mountains in the west. The man put an arm around the girl´s shoulders and brought his head close to hers. A long and expected kiss merged them. Debbie breathed a sigh of happiness at the perfect setting of the scene. She knew she would remember that moment for years and looked at the man with a broad smile that was enough reward for him. A long time passed in silence, respecting the majesty of nature.

"I'm starting to feel cold." Deborah finally said. "We better go back."

When they returned to the perimeter of the tents, the natural light was quickly extinguishing and the fire was reduced to embers.

Dennis pointed in the direction of Selma's tent and Debbie made a faint sound.

" It's Martín! He's getting into my sister's tent!"

"I suppose he has her consent. Otherwise we would already be hearing her cries."

"But she swore in front of me she would keep him at bay. She was furious to see him gawking at the Mongolian girl."

"Perhaps she has changed her mind. At that age the hormones press hard."

"You excuse your cousin very quickly. There are no guarantees that he will leave Selma chasing some Eskimo, Martian or some other female."

"That will also depend on Selma. Don 't you think?"

Chapter 27

The coordinates provided by the baron's diary marked an accumulation rocks in front of them. The position of the star that Selma had pointed out the night before coincided with that location. The fact that the data matched reinforced a feeling of success for having reached the goal that overwhelmed the travelers. That night only the Tibetan guides and Selma could sleep, the first because they hardly knew the purposes of the expedition, in their eyes only another extravagance of wealthy foreigners who did not need to work to earn their livelihood. As for the girl, she slept peacefully after the effort of concentration and of climbing of the mountain. The rest of the contingent remained awake despite themselves and the rays of the sun that emerged over the eastern summits found them drowsy and anxious.

The route they had to do on foot was about a mile in a straight line, but according to what they had already learned on their mountain experiences that distance would triple by the twists and turns of the path to follow. The whole route would be uphill, with a gentle slope at the beginning and steeper at the end; the ascent would not include mountaineering sections though but would be exclusively a trekking activity implying a good deal of effort. At times the path would force them to descend so that the difficulties would increase when they needed to recover that height.

Jack and Dennis alternated in the vanguard while Debbie and Selma traveled accompanied by Martín, and Maggie and Dieter closed the march in a column that stretched at times but oscillated in about fifty steps long. They often had to stop to allow the Debbie and Dieter to catch their breath.

"Remember to rehydrate frequently." reiterated Jack, veteran in marches in wild landscapes under the action of the sun.

They had already climbed two thirds of the altitude of the steep cliff and from then on they had to pay particular attention to all the details of the outline that could mark the entrance to a cave, an excavation, a practicable path or any other indication that looked striking and stood out from the rocky landscape, since von Ungern's diary did not describe the place they were looking for, since the Baron had never been there and only knew its location by hearsay. Dennis, who was in charge of the group at that moment, pointed to a small plain that opened to their right and said.

"We are going to make one last stop here before undertaking the assault to the top. Do not forget that we are going up the north wall but the entrance may be on any other side so it is possible that we should go around the summit to find it."

They all sat on the floor of the plateau, partially covered by patches of snow. After a while Dieter approached the cliff where the rock extension ended and peeked into the depths. Maggie came up behind him, overcoming her natural vertigo and aversion to emptiness. To avoid startling him, she spoke to the German when she was still several steps away.

" Do you see something strange or out of place?"

"A few flashes down there in the valley, mixed with the reflection of the snow." replied, Dieter pointing with his gloved finger towards the depths. The woman looked in the direction indicated and nodded, asking.

" Do you think that ...?

"No! In no way can it be what we are looking for. It's relatively far from the coordinates and it's on the stone floor." He pulled away and called Dennis out loud.

" Can you bring me those high-powered binoculars you have?"

Attracted by the call Dennis and Jack approached them, each one with binoculars. Dieter pointed in the direction of the distant object. The binoculars circulated among all without letting them establish the identity of what they were observing. Finally Jack recovered his lenses and looked at the site once again taking advantage of the fact that some clouds that were blocking the sun light momentarily moved away and exclaimed.

"I've got it!"

" Do you know what it is?"

" Yes. No doubt." He turned around and looked at his anxious companions.

"Those are the remains of a crashed plane at the bottom of the valley. Surely a small plane and as I can see from here, a pretty old artifact."

"We'll have to settle for that assumption." Dennis said." We cannot even think about getting closer to checking what you say! It is too far and deep."

The others nodded and then everyone returned to the landing where Martín was with the sisters, who were already getting ready to continue the march.

"Let's get on the road." Dennis said enthusiastically. "Our goal is a couple of hours away."

At that moment there was a dull thud that circulated through the valleys and they immediately recognized.

" It's a helicopter. Maybe the Chinese aircraft that already detected us." Said Jack. "Can you see it?"

"There, to the west." said Martín excited. "Now it's behind the top of that hill ... but there it reappears."

Indeed, everyone was able to visualize the machine because of the brightness of the sunlight on the fuselage.

"You think they have seen us?"

"I cannot know. If they did not see us already they may still see next depending on how they maneuver."

As if responding to the comment, the aircraft turned to 90 degrees, which changed the sound to a lower frequency due to the Doppler-Fizeau effect.

"It is moving away." Debbie exclaimed with a tone of relief.

"There is no doubt that they are on our track, but for now they look for us somewhere else."

"Let´s keep going." Dennis reiterated.

The route was complicated by the cliffs that appeared in the ascending road and that forced them to zigzag permanently and climb dangerous stretches in which behind them there was only an abyss. Each time all travelers reached a narrow strip of horizontal rock they took advantage of the safe position to catch their breath, which at that point was panting from the thin air.

"We have about three hundred feet vertically to reach the top." said Jack.

"Over there." Selma exclaimed, pointing to a point on the opposite side of the mountain. They all looked in that direction and saw that oddly the site was at a lower altitude than the one they were in.

" Let me go explore." said Dieter, who was the one with the most mountain training because of his excursions in the Alps of southern Germany. He moved away and disappeared from sight behind a bend in the hillside. A tense wait followed as the travelers were suspended in a narrow strip of rock and the wind began to blow from the east, endangering their precarious balance. After an agonizingly long time, Dieter reappeared behind the bend and motioned for the others to follow him. Fortunately, once the threatening bend was left behind the path widened as it descended so that the walking turned easier.

"There is something ahead, which can be the entrance to a cave." said Dieter.

Another two hundred steps beyond a dark sector on the slope marked what could be an entrance in front of a landing to which everyone could finally access. A stream of fresh air flowed from the site.

"This is definitely an access to a cave." Said the German, who always led the march. "I will go inside and let you know if we can safely enter it."

The remaining expedition members sat around the entrance of the presumed cave and took the time to rest and rehydrate without saying a word to save their breath. After a quarter of an hour the explorer reappeared once more and said.

"This is a scabrous opening to a cave system, whose main entrance must be elsewhere. We must definitely enter. Once the first section is over and the central tunnel is reached, the journey will be easier."

They moved in the deep darkness, only broken by Jack's flashlight, since he had now taken the lead. Although they all carried flashlights they refrained from using them at the same time to save batteries. As they descended the tunnel was effectively becoming wider and higher, allowing also Jack and Dennis, both tall men, to walk upright.

"*Herr Direktor.* We are already in front of the planned site. We have already visualized the entrance to the cave and are prepared to enter."

"All right. Have you seen any sign of Berglund and his people?"

"Back down we have found signs of a camp and traces of several vehicles, maybe three."

Wildau made a moment of silence and then asked the question he had been holding.

" If this is really the place, there is no problem that we enter with the Chinese?"

"Get in with the whole troop. From a moment that you must determine yourself, you will only go ahead with the officer ... what is her name?"

"Liu, Liu Daiyu.

"Liu. Tell me, how is she?"

"Very efficient."

"And what are her looks? You know, my secretary Gerda, who knows your Casanova fame is jealous. She cannot conceive that you prefer a Chinese woman rather than an Aryan."

Wildau blushed so he was glad that his superior could not see him. The problem was not the womanizer's fame that he had, which was well known to the Director, but the fact that the boss knew about his relationship-in reality purely sexual- with Gerda Schmiddel.

"Daiyu is very pretty." He conceded and changed the subject. "We are ready to start."

"Keep me informed." added the Director before cutting off the communication.

Wildau approached Daiyu and his men, who were checking the state of their weapons. The German took out his Gluck pistol from its holster and did his own verification. Then he looked at the woman and said curtly.

"Let's go then. From a certain point on just only you and me will follow."

" Yes, I have also received instructions."

Wildau wondered how it was possible for the Director to share decisions on such a sensitive issue with the Chinese military. He shook his head, knowing there were things he would never have access to, such as the link between the heirs of the Third Reich and sectors of the supposedly Communist Chinese People's Army.

After exploring several side tunnels that ended in stone walls the travelers walked along the main corridor that was slowly widening; the air was fresh, as if somewhere there were ventilation holes through which it could get renewed. Jack stayed at the front of the group and those who marched behind had also lit their lamps in order to examine the walls and corners of the corridor to avoid possible objects of interest go unnoticed.

In a moment Jack stopped and as the remaining group members approached him they saw the reason for his perplexity. Two equally wide tunnels opened to the left and right and when illuminated by the torches they seemed equally deep.

"I do not know which to follow." said Jack in a low voice to Dennis who was at his side.

"At this point we must make a decision. We cannot divide our group to explore both because we could be isolated in the belly of the mountain and never meet again."

At that moment the rest of the contingent joined them and unexpectedly Selma went forward entering the corridor that opened to the right.

"Here. This is the way." Said with certainty without looking if the others followed her.

" Wait, Selma! Do not go alone."Debbie yelled after her sister. The rest of the group had no choice but to follow them to avoid being divided, so the young woman determined the direction to follow of the entire expedition based on her intuition, without leaving room for evaluations or hesitations.

"I hope that your sister's hunch is correct this time too." whispered Dennis in Deborah's ear.

" Until now she has not failed and has taken us out of several troubles. Anyway, do you have a better idea?" She answered in a defiant tone, so the man chose not to answer.

Chapter 28

Wildau and Daiyu led the platoon that was advancing through the narrow tunnel. At one point one of the soldiers pointed his lamp to the ground and exclaimed something in Chinese. The woman bent down and picked up a small cylinder from the floor.

" Hans, look at this." She said, displaying a flashlight battery in his hand.

"It is evident that this place was recently visited." answered the German. "We are on the right path. Tell your men to prepare their weapons, we can run into the group we are following."

"Remember that there were no vehicles downstairs. If they were here, they have likely left."

"We are at the coordinates that my boss indicated. The data comes from a good source. Whether they are in this cave at this moment or not we are following their footsteps closely." Wildau was obviously excited. Although the Director had never explicitly stated to him what they were looking for, he knew that it was one of the great secrets of the last sixty or seventy years. Wildau was not only moved by the desire for success and reward that a finding of that nature could generate, but above all for serving what he considered his duty. The military contingent continued its way extreme precautions and observing the strictest silence.

Gerda Schmiddel tapped the heavy door with her knuckles and entered the large office.

"*Herr Direktor*, you have a call in the private room."

"Thanks Gerda. Hold any other calls and cancel appointments for the next half hour."

The man stood up, took a tablet that was on the desk and after a moment of hesitation he put it back in its place and took instead a paper notebook. Although he was technologically updated, the Director entrusted important topics to traditional media. He went to the small reserved room and lifted the telephone tube. After the protocol greetings, he directly entered the subject because he knew that his interlocutor appreciated conciseness.

" My people are already in the place whose coordinates Berglund informed his Bluthund superiors. I am expectant and with high hopes."

"I hope you're right Helmut. You know well the importance of knowing the precise location of that site. We lost that information more than fifty years ago, when the plane that brought von Schirach and his lieutenant back to Berlin crashed somewhere in the Himalaya taking the secret with them."

" How did they not send the data by some other additional means, as a backup? Such information cannot be entrusted to a single emissary, a certain degree of redundancy is essential."

"You know that the means at that time were more precarious than the current ones. In addition, the information had to be kept with maximum secrecy, which implied that only very few people could have access to it. On the other hand, it is true that information management protocols have evolved since then, but unfortunately that is the real situation now."

"What else do we know about the site?"

"Only the location in very general terms in that area of Tibet. We know from the last communications of von Schirach that the cave system has several entrances although he did not get to explore them all."

"I do not understand why that valuable cargo was carried to that remote part of the planet."

" You know the theories of the origin of the Aryan race in the subterranean city of Agartha and its surroundings. The instructions that the top leaders had left were to return to the sources."

While advancing in front of the group Jack felt a slight current of air brushing his cheek. From previous experiences he already knew that this boasted the existence of openings in the mountain ahead of them somehow connected with the tunnel through which they walked. The finger of light from his flashlight showed him that on the further down the path twisted to the left so that there was only a stone wall in front of him. When arriving at the bend in the breeze a sense of freshness reached the skin of his face and hands. As he directed the beam of light in the new direction an exhalation came out of his mouth.

"What's wrong, Jack?" asked Dennis who was immediately following him. The aforementioned pointed his index finger towards the front.

A REFLECTION OF WATER was perceived before them in a sudden widening of the path that eventually led to a large pond filled entirely with the liquid. Only on one side a series of stones emerging from the waters advanced in them but it could not be determined a priori if it reached the other end of the lake, which was barely discernible in the prevailing darkness. The dark water volume projected a somewhat sinister image that exerted a depressive psychological effect on the explorers as they arrived.

"This water surely leaks from the outside somewhere." Dennis' voice startled his partner. "It is not impossible that there is another entrance to this tunnel behind the lake."

"I'll try to get around it walking with the rocks." answered Jack. "We'll see if they reach the other side. If it does, we will walk over them one at a time to avoid surprises."

Saying that, he took the backpack off his back and handed it to Dennis.

"Hold it. I'm going to try to walk over the edge to the other side to test if it's feasible to arrive safely and then I'll come back."

MEANWHILE, THE OTHER travelers had reached the shore of the lake and watched in amazement the unexpected spectacle. The last one to approach was Selma, who from the first moment was unsettled by the dark surface of the waters; her sister, noticing her condition took her arm trying to push her away saying.

"Now we are going to try to cross to the other side, but if you do not want to go you and me will stay here, waiting for the return of the others.

The girl exclaimed in distress pointing to the interior of the lake.

"No, no! That's where we have to go."

" You mean at the bottom of the water pond?"

Selma nodded and added.

"I know it sounds bizarre, but I have a very strong intuition. We have to look down there."

They all looked at the girl rather bewildered, not wanting to contradict her out loud; finally Dieter expressed the general feeling.

"Do you mean that what we are looking for is at the bottom of this lake? You realize that it sounds very unlikely."

"I do not know how it can be explained." answered Selma. "I only feel a strong attraction to that place."

The silence extended in the group since in this case to follow the intuitions of the young person entailed a concrete danger; then suddenly Martín exclaimed.

"I offer myself to explore the depths of the lake. I am a good swimmer and diver and I have great ability to retain air."

"You expose yourself to an unknown danger." Argued Dieter. "The well can be very deep and is totally dark."

In that moment Jack returned with the news that crossing the lake walking over the stones was impossible since they did not reach the other shore.

" So the only possibility left is the one Selma indicates." concluded Dennis.

" Until the moment the visions of Selma have been successful." answered Martín. " The only way to verify the veracity this time is to submerge."

Seeing that his relative was determined Dennis took part in the debate.

"I have a waterproof flashlight and you Jack have a very long rope. We will tie it to Martín's waist." Then he warned. " But Martín, when you get to the end of the rope you come back. Have you understood me?"

The young man took off his clothes and was only covered by his underpants. Then tied the rope around his waist according to the request of his relative and prepared to dive into the water when Selma suddenly jumped on him, put her arms around him and tiptoed to kiss him in the mouth.

"Wow! It seems your sister has regrets for having been the one with the idea." whispered Dennis in his girlfriend's ear.

"Rather, I think she overcame her inhibition and did what she wanted to do in public for a while." Then she turned to Selma and said, "That's enough, let Martín plunge before he changes his mind."

Martín put one foot in the water to feel its temperature. A shiver ran through his body. However, without thinking, he threw himself into the dark liquid.

The icy water at the same time limited the movements of the swimmer and made him move more energetically to overcome the numbness. The finger of light of the torch marked him in his descent the rocky outline of the well to the abyssal depths of the bottom. Martín spent a few moments trying to get oriented and when he did not succeed to do it decided to return to the surface to breathe again. To his despair he found that he could not find the way back while the air and his lungs were already bursting with oppression. With a last ray of lucidity the boy thought he saw the light of the exit on one side and there swam with boldness.

When his head emerged into the dark cavity above the water level Martín was already almost unconscious. He tried to support one foot in a stony protuberance and affirm himself there. He was surprised at the absence of light and noise in space, since he had imagined finding his friends waiting for him. He picked up the flashlight attached to his waist. It was off but luckily shaking it a bit managed to turn it on again. When he directed the beam of light in all directions, he found with astonishment that it was not in the same place where he had submerged but in a very wide enclosure of which the torch did not illuminate the end. He confirmed he was alone in the place and could not hear any sound except those produced by himself as he emerged. Laboriously he came out of the water finding a rock floor covered with sand. The contact with the cold air made him sneeze and tremble while his teeth chattered. He made several push-ups to put the blood back into circulation, and then walked a few steps guided by the light. The boy soon realized that there was a vast stone enclosure in front of him and there he directed the beam of light.

The scene that opened before his eyes left Martín petrified with amazement.

Chapter 29

Selma walked around the perimeter of the lagoon, in a growing nervousness. The other expedition members were also expectant and a bit alarmed for the delay of Martín but they tried to control their anxiety so as not to mortify the young woman even more. In a moment the girl emitted a series of sobs and finally a scream. Dennis tugged on the rope that had been tied around Martín's waist to maintain physical contact with him and realized desperately that the rope was loose and could be picked up effortlessly; when they reached its end the travelers could see that it was frayed.

"The rope is cut, probably by the friction against the rock." Mused Dennis in contained voice. The despair began to invade the companions of the absent youth.

"I should never have let him get into that dark pit." added Dennis in a plaintive voice.

"It's no use to blame yourself." answered Jack putting a hand on his comrade's shoulder. He was going to add something else when there was a new scream from Selma. They all turned to her and were surprised to see the look on her face.

"He could get out of the water!" Said the girl with bright eyes.

"But where is he? What are you talking about?" Her sister answered worriedly.

"I do not know, but it's in a big, dark place. I only know that it's a cold spot, very cold."

One of the soldiers uttered an exclamation in Chinese, while illuminating with his lamp the side wall of the tunnel. Fixed to it was a metallic object embedded in the cracks of the stone. Wildau came over and said to Daiyu.

"It is a hook to hang ancient lanterns, of those that worked with kerosene or other petroleum derivatives. There is no doubt that we are on the right path. Whether Berglund and his people are in front of us or not we are in the right place. The woman looked at him in the face and was impressed by the brightness of his eyes.

Guided by the dim light of the torch, whose battery was evidently close to being exhausted, Martín walked through the interior of the room. At the moment he could not understand well what it was that emitted those metallic reflections but tried to record it well in his memory to be able to transmit it to his friends... in case he could meet them again.

Martín directed the light back to the well of water from which he had emerged and could barely overcome the terror that the idea of diving back into him to return produced. He walked a few steps and soon felt in his face a slight current of cold air. Even though he was struggling against freezing, the breeze seemed a good omen, since as he had learned in previous cave experiences during the long trip, it would eventually lead to an exit to the outside of the mountain. He walked another hundred steps following the current of air and suddenly found that the tunnel ended abruptly in a chaos of loose rocks that could not be removed with his hands. Evidently a collapse had cut the course of the passage at some indeterminable moment. He exhaled a plaintive moan when assessing his situation, lost in the bowels of the mountain, separated from his friends and completely naked. At that moment the battery of the lamp completely spent its charge and Martín went dark. He leaned his head against the stone wall and wept bitterly. After the breakdown serenity slowly returned to his spirit and inside him the decision was generated not to let himself be overcome by the situation and take charge of his destiny.

In a moment he raised his head and visualized something he could not pin down. He rubbed his eyes and looked again at the roof of the tunnel; a star appeared as if painted in a black sky.

Hoping that the opening through which the solitary light filtered through was wide enough to allow him to pass through it without waiting for a moment he rushed the almost vertical wall of rock to be able to climb out of his mineral enclosure. In his ascent he paid no attention to the innumerable injuries that the stone produced on his bare skin and holding on to his legs and arms he finally emerged on the mountainside. The icy air hit him and being exposed naked to its action of the wind became unbearable but he immediately went into a nook to wait for the sun to rise. He thought that the side of the mountain on which he stood was facing east, so that with the first light of dawn the sun's rays would warm his body; the essential thing was to stay alive until then.

In spite of the external cold a certain pride warmed his interior. To have been able to overcome the confinement in the well had been in the first place a conquest of courage and commitment in front of extremely adverse circumstances. Although Martín was not yet aware of the transformation, a boy had thrown himself into the waters of the lagoon but a man had left his confinement in the mountain.

In addition, he had left the mountain prison having a new piece of knowledge as overwhelming as bizarre.

DESPITE THE FATIGUE Hans Wildau and Liu Daiyu were almost running inside the long tunnel. Obeying the instructions given by the Director, they had left the rest of the troop of soldiers behind, with orders to wait for them in a kind of wide chamber formed by the action of remote waters in the passageway. The certainty of approaching the goal had triggered the chief's recommendation of confidentiality and it was also clear that the expedition organized by Bluthund was no longer in the tunnel, so it was not a danger for which the soldiers were needed. What they were going to find was only for the eyes of the German and the Chinese captain, who apparently had the approval of the Director. Ahead of them was the umpteenth corner of the tunnel and Wildau's expectation was to meet at any time the object of their quest, whatever its nature, but certainly a determining factor for the durability of the Third Reich and its eventual transformation into a Fourth Reich of the 21st century.

The reality that was hidden behind the bend was overwhelming; a crumbling had created an impenetrable rock wall. Wildau muttered a curse and hit the stone wall with his fist. His dreams of glory collapsed in an instant and he fell to his knees on the floor of the small chamber that faced the wall. Distressed to see the man's reaction and proceeding in a way that surprised even her, Daiyu knelt beside him and took his head in her arms. Thus, on the floor of a corridor in the bowels of a mountain lost in Tibet and consoled by a Chinese woman, the fierce warrior of the Aryan race burst into tears.

After a prolonged time in that position, Daiyu brought her lips close to the man's and both joined in a prolonged kiss, produced not only by sexual desire but by a feeling that none of them had experienced before. In an extremely unresponsive place and in the middle of a deep disappointment, instead of the legacy of the Nazis Hans Wildau found love.

They both remained embraced in the dim light of the lamp until Daiyu prepared to stand up. As she did so, her foot stumbled over something that was buried in the sandy soil, exposing it. Filled with curiosity the woman picked the object up and exposed it to the light of the lantern.

" It's a bone." Said Wildau." Possibly cranial."

"But it is very thick." answered the woman." It looks like part of a bear skull."

The memories of stories of expeditions to Tibet heard in his childhood returned to the mind of the German.

"Look." said Daiyu. "Here the sand on the soil is scrambled. It is obvious that someone excavated here. Notice this, another piece of bone. Berglund and his people have surely been here."

Wildau shook his head as if to clear his ideas. After all, maybe they would not leave the cave empty-handed.

They all looked desolate. Dennis had plunged into the inner lake and dived as far as his forces had allowed but had found no trace of his relative and emerged with his body frozen. The information baffled the members of the expedition, with the odd exception of Selma who seemed relatively calm. Finally Jack made the decision.

" There is no point in continuing desperate here in this dismal environment. Let´s return to the camp outside the cave, there we will think with a fresh head and plan to return to this lake by bringing means to wade it."

" Are there any inflatable rafts on the trucks?"

"Yes, we have a small one. The hypothesis of crossing a watercourse had been analyzed when we made preparations for the expedition."

"We better wait to go outside until dawn ." added Dieter. "We have to descend the steep slope and there's no sense in risking falling in the darkness."

The decision taken by consensus was then to return to the mouth of the cave and wait there for the first morning light.

"YOU TELL ME THERE WERE traces of recent activity in the cave?" The Director had received in silence the exposure that Wildau had made through the secure telephone line about the finding on the site whose coordinates he had provided. Taking over the discouragement of the subordinate by the frustrated search, the Director had reacted in a pragmatic way and tried to reconstruct what happened to make decisions.

"Yes. The floor of the rock chamber had been disturbed and still excavated, no doubt recently.

"You say you sent me pictures of the bones found?"

"Yes. Look for them on your cell phone, you should have received them already."

"Hold on one moment."

The boss walked to his main office, where the mobile phone was placed in his desk and confirmed the reception of the photographs. He took time to observe them and then returned to the reserved room and continued the conversation with his subordinate.

"Well, it could be that the theories that motivated the Schäffer expedition to Tibet in 1938 were not so crazy after all. Have you kept those bones?"

"Yes. I have them with me. In total there are seven pieces. I do not think there's any more left. With Dai ... with Captain Liu we have searched exhaustively."

"Well done. Listen out. It is obvious that the Bluthund expedition has found the same as you and that they have an time advantage. But they have not terminated their search because otherwise I would have already learned about it through my contacts, so they should have another clue. I'm going to ask my Chinese friends to take extra vigilance of the area from the air and locate them again. The tracking area is more limited now and I trust they will find them. Wait for my call. Meanwhile you can search yourself around that spot...with your Chinese captain, I mean."

Wildau thought he sensed an unaccustomed air of scorn in his superior.

The first lights of the morning had already appeared. The travelers had arrived at the camp, and after taking a short break they had prepared the equipment to start a second trial this time duly prepared to cross the lake. They were ready to get going when the Tibetan guides began to talk excitedly pointing to the side of the mountain. Dennis was talking to Jack and Debbie when they heard the rumor.

" Have you marked properly on the map ...? But what the hell happens?"

Deborah was startled to see her sister run towards the base of the mountain.

"Wait Selma. Where...? Oh God!"

All were staring at the slope along which a human figure was descending with difficulty. A formidable Hurray emerged from all the throats in unison.

When all the members of the expedition arrived at where Selma was, she was embraced by a completely naked Martín with his skin covered with bleeding sores and a weak but smiling appearance. Dennis was the first to arrive and touching the skin of his relative shouted.

"He is frozen! Soon, we have to avoid hypothermia. Although the sun has already dawned, the morning is freezing. Light a large fire and prepare blankets and hot tea."

The Tibetan guides had brought a collapsible stretcher in which they deposited Martín and immediately the delegation returned to the camp and its members approached the fire they had effectively lit. Even before healing the wounds on the young man's body, they proceeded to vigorously rub his skin to restore blood circulation and then wrap him in blankets and keep him close to the fire.

Returning to his own camp with the rest of the troop, Liu Daiyu and Wildau went directly to the woman's tent. Both were infatuated with the reciprocal feelings that had manifested in the cavern at a time when frustration had lowered the armor that normally covered both warriors. These feelings were an experience unknown to them and in reality they had to learn how to handle them. Hans Wildau was conscious that they had to prepare the next step for the moment he received instructions from his boss, but for the first time in his life he decided to postpone his obligations to attend his feelings. Throughout the day the lovers did not leave their tent, generating smiles and brief comments from the Chinese soldiers.

The night had fallen and it was notorious the improvement of Martín's physical condition. Selma had been in the tent all day, warming with her own body the young man's lying next to her in a sleeping bag. Finally both emerged from the tent and approached the fire around which the other comrades were already gathered. The phrases of all were of warm reception to the boy. After dinner Dennis asked his cousin if he was in a position to narrate what happened. Martín was slowly trying to organize his partial and somewhat unconnected memories.

"You say there's another outlet to the surface near the lake?" asked Dennis. "I did not see her when I submerged in your search."

"I found it by chance when there was no more air left... it was a sort of lifeline...."

"I was terrified and disoriented and I had to travel a great distance underwater."

"Can you describe what you found in that place you were in?" Jack was asking the questions now.

"The light of my flashlight was weak and finally the battery ran out. What I could see was a large room, very spacious, with relatively flat floor and walls and a rather high ceiling. The only object that I could distinguish inside before the light was finished was a kind of ... sarcophagus or something like that."

The statement produced stupor in the listeners.

"It looked like those of the mummies in the pyramids of Egypt?" asked Debbie.

" No, it rather looked as those I saw in a documentary about the tombs of the ancient kings of Spain in the Monastery of El Escorial, near Madrid. A kind of monumental and lavish construction."

" Made in marble?"

"Maybe partially but it also had metal parts. I remember the brightness reflected in the light of the torch. Keep in mind that I could see all this in a very fleeting way."

The comment with the strange comparison with imperial tombs produced puzzlement as well as excitement among those present. The afternoon had already fallen and everyone was tired so Jack decided to close the discussion.

" Tomorrow we'll to take a rest day and we will make the preparations to go to the pond. Do you think you'll be able to join us?" He asked addressing Martín.

"Hope so. I want to be able to determine what I really saw."

The travelers had transported all the equipment to the tunnel and had taken it to the edge of the lagoon. There they finished inflating the raft and threw it into the dark waters. Jack, Dennis and Dieter got on board with some of that equipment and when they left the first one shouted at the other travelers.

"We are going to explore the other side of the lagoon and if everything goes well we will go back to look for you. I figure that in two more trips we can transport all of you."

From that moment began a long wait for those who remained on the shore. They were already used to these periods of calm that worked as anti-climaxes among others of intense activity.

A couple of hours had passed and they finally saw that the raft was coming back out of the darkness of the lagoon. It surprised them that the three men came on board, and not just Dieter, as they had agreed.

"What happened? Why are you back?" asked Debbie.

"The tunnel on the other side of the pond is completely blocked by debris." answered Dennis as he got off the raft and walked through the water.

"It seems that all the corridors of the mountain are blocked by landslides." commented Martín.

"It is not surprising. Tibet suffers frequent and very destructive earthquakes, of magnitude 7 on the Richter scale or even higher. In particular in 1950 and in 2015 there were two earthquakes with thousands of victims. The Himalaya are young mountains that have arisen from friction between the Asian and Indian tectonic plates and are in full growth, of course in extensive geological periods. It is because of that youth that they are the highest mountain ranges in the world."

"Is this the end of our search?" asked Maggie.

"Of course not. We have the alternative to go directly to the room where Martín was and enter the mountain through the hole he used to get outside. Is it a practicable way?" He asked, addressing the boy.

"Yes, it is a very high exit and we'll have to ascend a wall with a steep slope, but it's nothing we have not done already."

" Can we all go?

"With a careful preparation, yes. We are already trained in this type of mountaineering."

The expedition members stepped back and reached the outside of the mountain. There they rested a while Martín looked on the slope trying to ascertain the way he had used the day before to go downhill. Once he had located the path just outlined between the rocks he returned with his comrades. At that moment a buzzing sound that had already become familiar was heard. Everyone peered into the sky in search of the source of the noise and it was finally Maggie who spotted it. As they presumed, it was indeed a helicopter flying over nearby summits until it finally disappeared behind them.

"Do you think they have spotted us?" asked Selma.

"I hope not, but let's not delude ourselves. It can only be a Chinese aircraft and as we already know from experience they are permanently in our search." replied Jack somberly. " If we do not finish our search and leave this area soon they will surely find us, it is only a matter of time."

The satellite phone rang and Wildau hurriedly answered the call, knowing who was the only one who could call. He left the tent to speak freely with a notebook and a pencil. He returned after a few minutes and deposited everything in his backpack.

"Any news?" asked Daiyu.

"It was my boss. Your people located Berglund and his crew. I already have the coordinates."

Chapter 30

The climb was more difficult than expected. Martín had indeed made the same trip two days before in an almost delirious state but in a downward direction, so to travel in the opposite direction consumed much more energy and time. Finally they arrived at a breach in the rock that the young man identified as his place of exit; again in the light of day he was able to verify the tricks memory plays since according to it the entrance was wider than it ultimately turned out to be.

Once inside the passage the task of the group became easier, since this time the direction was downward and they walked with the light of several lamps, avoiding the damages inflicted on Martín's body by the rocks of sharp contours. Also the length of the corridor was greater than what was recorded by his memory but finally they arrived at a place where the tunnel widened and the roof moved up allowing everyone to walk in an upright position.

"We are near now." Said the young man, who was marching to the front.

"What is this? " Asked Jack pointing to a corridor that opened laterally.

"We are not interested in it. We must always continue forward." Martín exclaimed excitedly assaulted suddenly by his memories. "Oh, there it is! That is the place!"

Indeed the lanterns illuminated a great expansion in the rock forming an enclosure of considerable dimensions, although no object was seen inside it.

"There is! That is the same lagoon that you already know from the other side." Martín exclaimed, jumping to the edge of the dark well; it was obvious that the boy was subjected to violent emotions. "I arrived here! This exit to open air saved my life."

Everyone could see the cavity full of liquid, much smaller in size than the opening in the same lagoon that they already knew located in the other tunnel.

" So, by the principle of communicating vessels, we are at the same altitude as the other entrance to the lake on the path we already know." explained Dennis.

"But where is the sarcophagus or whatever it was you called that way?" Questioned Jack.

Martín moved away from the water's edge and after orienting himself in the enclosure ran to one side and illuminated the spot with his torch and then everyone saw it.

Dieter approached as if hypnotized. He reacted immediately and putting on disposable gloves slid his hands over the polished surface leaving the trace of his hand in the dust removed.

The others moved slowly around the marble block, interrogating it with their eyes. Dennis began his meticulous filming work by moving slowly and gently pushing away his comrades who interfered in the visual; he then took pictures from different angles and finally took from his pocket a sketchbook where he had been drawing from the tunnel mouth their route inside the hill since the GPS did not work inside the mountain due to the lack of satellite signals. The American had taken over the entire task of documentation and geo-localization since the beginning of the expedition in the then distant Mongolia months ago. He was the only one who remained active while the rest of his comrades were still contemplative.

Deborah and Selma remained at a certain distance, feeling a certain instinctive rejection of the room and its presumed content, while Maggie extracted her cell phone with a recorder and as was her custom dictated an oral report of everything found.

<< The place has obviously been designed as a crypt or mausoleum. >> Dictated to the recorder. << and in its center there is a sepulcher of marble and steel, which has been properly described as similar to the tombs of European kings in El Escorial of Spain, Roskilde in Denmark and other similar ones. The execution is imposing but sober and there is no doubt that its purpose has been to house the remains of some character of the highest hierarchy. The style is fully European, very different from any Asian known tomb or monument and at first sight it is not possible to determine neither the character that lies there nor the time frame, although without danger to err it can be placed between the past 50 or 100 years. In view of the present arrangement of the caverns, it is inexplicable how an object of such a large volume has been

brought into this enclosure sunk so inaccessibly into the mountain. It can only be assumed that it was transported through an easily accessible tunnel that totally or partially collapsed afterwards in the large earthquakes frequent in this region. The corridor through which we originally came and then found collapsed could maybe explain the location of the coffin in this place and even the formation of the lake that interrupts it may have happened later. On the marble top there is a steel swastika below which a legend in Gothic German is read ... Dieter Could you please translate it in front of the microphone?>>

The voice of the German recorded the enigmatic phrase << May you rest in the craddle of our ancestors, only worthy place for you. >>

Once her oral report was finished, Maggie interrupted the recording and sneaked up on Dieter.

"Who do you think is there? Do you think the same as me?"

"Frankly I cannot think of another character that would deserve this ritual burial."

"But ... the corpse found in the bunker along with that of Eva Braun ... then taken by the Russians ..."

"The body was burned with gasoline. The Russians gave unclear versions of what happened with the remains, and finally ... you know ... there have always been rumors that he was seen alive after the end of the Second World War in Argentina, Paraguay and other places. There is no totally suspicious-free version."

At that moment Debbie and Dennis approached, the first with a worried face.

" Selma is extremely restless. This site has completely removed her calmness."

Without answering him Dennis called Martín who came immediately.

" Take Selma away from this site. Go back to the camp." Before the doubtful gesture of his cousin added. "Later I will explain to you."

Once the boys have gone Dennis asked.

"Well, what is your conclusion regarding this place.

"We can only think of a Nazi hierarch about whose burial site there are doubts."

"You are talking about Hitler himself."

"Yes."

"And what about the history of suicide in the Berlin bunker?"

"There have always been doubts about it and versions of his survival." Maggie answered. "But even if he had died there, the whereabouts of his corpse was always controversial and there is no firm information on where it is."

Jack had joined the meeting and had overheard the Englishwoman´s last words.

"The revelation of these news can shake the world." He said. " And not for the better."

"Why?" Dennis asked. "If he's dead anyway."

"But he is still an iconic symbol of fans in many parts of the world. Turning this site into a Nazi cathedral would constitute a global revulsive. And let's not forget that it is in Chinese territory. I fail to even imagine what Beijing's reaction might be in this case."

"I cannot still believe that all this is true and that it is happening to us." Debbie's tone was uneasy.

"The fact that someone is looking for us in itself is symptomatic." added Jack." They are mobilizing important resources belonging to the Chinese People's Army."

"I cannot understand what the Nazis and the People's Republic of China have in common." said Dennis.

"The chances are that they have nothing in common." Maggie replied. "What happens is that there is a lot of corruption in China, and certain high-ranking military leaders tend to use the means that the army puts at their disposal for their own benefit . This occurs particularly in remote garrisons far from Beijing and the productive area of China and this may be one example."

"Even so. What is the link between these hierarchs and the Nazis?" Dennis insisted.

"In all likelihood it's money." replied the Englishwoman.

" What will we do? I do not want to put Selma and myself in the middle of a Nazi operation. There are relatives of my parents who died in Dachau." Tears rolled down Debbie's cheeks.

"I think it's best to document all our findings and leave this place as soon as possible." said Jack

"You mean to end the expedition?" Asked Dieter.

" Yes, but as a success story, not as a failure, although it may never be disclosed what we have found. I do not think Bluthund has ever been involved in anything so big."

"And so dangerous." added Dennis.

" But what right do we have to hide from the world such relevant information?"

"The decision will not be made by us but the Executive Committee of the Bluthund Community. There are very powerful people from all over the world who have a broad view of the repercussions that this finding may have, and also have the wisdom to judge it." Jack spoke with a tone that reflected a certain thrill.

"You have a great emotional bond with Bluthund. pointed Debbie with her usual insight.

"It's my second homeland." acknowledged Jack. "What we must do at the moment is to promise not to divulge to anyone what happened this evening on this site, or its location, until we receive instructions of Bluthund's directors."

"Don't forget that I belong to MI6, I will have to report all our activities to my bosses." Maggie argued.

"Fair enough. They have been co-sponsors of this expedition along with Bluthund."

"We hope that there is no conflict of interest between the two." Reflected Dennis soberly.

"Let's go now and remember not to make any comments to the Tibetan guides. We must also include Selma and Martín in the silence pact that we have agreed upon."

The two youngsters arrived at the camp where the Tibetan drivers were cleaning their clothes and preparing their food. Two of the men wielded strange string instruments with which they produced a continuous and rhythmic melody. The girl had already recovered from the disturbance that the explicit and hidden contents of the crypt had produced in her psyche and both had been walking along the last stretch of the road holding hands; the young couple had exchanged few words as if they had agreed to limit the dialogue to the essential. As they arrived at the camp instead of going to the tents or to the fire lit by the guides Selma led the boy to some low rocks where they could sit. The night was falling rapidly and the new moon allowed the shining of thousands of stars to illuminate the landscape with their faint light. Selma looked up as Martín followed her gaze.

"Look." Said the girl pointing with her index finger in a vertical direction above their heads. "Do you see that star up there?"

"I see a star brighter than the others. I do not know what star it is."

"That has been and will be our guiding star. The star of Agartha."

Wildau, Liu Daiyu and their companions had finally discovered the entrance to the cavern whose location had been provided by the crew of the Chinese People's Army helicopter and had entered with great expectations to explore it. At many time zones of distance the Director, after giving Gerda Schmiddel the authorization to retire due to the late hour, had taken off his shoes and had settled into a spacious three-seat armchair waiting for the call of his subordinate, which also produced to him an anxiety that he had not experienced in a long time. In reality, all the indications concurred to suggest that they were already close to elucidating the mystery of the location of the great relic, whose finding duly handled by the propaganda apparatus they still had could serve to mobilize the dormant energies in the masses of many potential followers, discontented with the systems of government that predominated now in the world based on democracy and liberal capitalism. An old sacred fire that supposedly came from the genes of the race was about to resurrect passions long repressed since the end of the Second World War. With that on mind the Director tried to prevent falling asleep in his chair, although his tired body would require it; even so, he could not overcome the numbness encouraged by the absolute absence of sounds from the reserved room and the tenuous overhead light he had left on.

An insistent ringing ripped him out of his sleep and the start caused his feet to fall from the chair. Nervously he put on his glasses and pounced on the satellite phone that was on the small table.

"Hello! Yes, tell me Hans."

The old man's disappointment was enormous when his acolyte told him the long journey through the tunnel, the surprise of finding a lake in front of them interrupting their passage, as they had been able to ford it with small inflatable boats, and the final and definitive frustration in finding the way beyond the lake completely blocked by a great landslide undoubtedly of seismic origin.

The Director felt that his great hope was also collapsing and he took some time to process the news and handle the disenchantment. After a few moments of silence on the telephone line Wildau said ruefully.

" I'm sorry, Herr Direktor. I could not do more."

"Oh, no, no Hans! You have done a magnificent job. We have not yet found what we are looking for but we know almost exactly where it is. If you cannot find more data in the field, prepare your return home."

Once the call with Wildau ended, the Director dialed another phone. He was not surprised to find that his interlocutor was also awake and anxious, so he had attended the call to the second sound of the bell. The man named Otto listened attentively and also had a moment of frustration. Then he asked.

" What do you think the members of the Bluthund expedition have done?"

"We are sure that they have arrived at the same place, and obviously they have found the same as we did."

Then Otto reacted in the same way that the Director had done before. This common reaction was based on the ideological coincidence and the long chain of defeats and disappointments that they had experienced.

"Don't worry, Helmut. We have not found it now, but for the first time since von Schirach and his men fell with their plane, we know quite precisely where it is. The progress is enormous. It's just a matter of time. With the right means, a rubble wall can be perforated. Just make sure Wildau has the exact coordinates of the place. We will be back!"

Epilogue

Jack had made contact with William Richardson, to whom he had narrated in detail all the news since the last call. When it was his turn to explain the contents of the crypt in the mountain, the princely tomb of marble and steel and the symbols on its lid, and to refer to the hypothesis about the personality of the occupant of the crypt, Richardson was not amazed as Jack would have expected, and instead he accepted the theory willingly.

"You do not seem very surprised." said Berglund.

"I'm not at this stage of events."

"How is that? A ghost reappears more than 60 years later and it is not news."

"I do not want to detract from the findings you have made; they are amazing. What happens is that when analyzing the actions of those who persecuted you and theorizing about their possible motives, the always debatable but always present possibility that Hitler's body would reappear was one of those we had considered."

"What should we do now?"

"Return home with the maximum secrecy and the highest priority. I will organize a meeting of the Directing Council of the Bluthund Community to be made within the next few days. I suppose that you have obtained a lot of filmed, photographed material and have fixed the coordinates of the site with precision."

"Of course."

"All right. Return to Beijing as soon as possible, be extremely discreet there. I suppose you have kept the Tibetan guides uninformed of the results."

"Yes. There is another matter. It's about Maggie Garland, from MI6. Obviously she is aware of everything."

" We are going to talk to her current bosses, who must be processing at this very moment a very unpleasant news that we had to notify them."

"What are you talking about?"

"I'll tell you in person when we meet in New York. Returning to Garland, I will try to have her bosses authorize her presence at our meeting. In the first part of it we will cover all those topics that she already knows. The same is true for Dieter von Eichenberg."

Sir David Osborne was in one of the armchairs in the great hall of his gentlemen's club in London. It was a select institution that only admitted military men and people linked to the British intelligence services, in a situation of retirement and with blades of unblemished services and in fact constituted the second home for the elderly. Sir David was reading the newspaper in his favorite place near a huge log fire and was deeply penetrated with his reading of the international news supplement. The latest information he had received was unsettling, although he knew that those news would not appear in the newspapers. Suddenly, one of the staff employees of the club approached him and very quietly told him.

"Sir David, can I bother you?"

The fact was anomalous, since the silence inside the room was broken only for extraordinary reasons.

"Yes, what do you need Butler?"

"Some gentlemen are waiting for you at the entrance of the room. They have requested you to kindly join them."

Sir David looked at the entrance and saw three men wearing waterproof trench coats and carrying their hats in their hands. He had momentarily a dizziness of nervous origin but he overcame it immediately. He knew perfectly well that he was downhill in his career and could well imagine what awaited him. He left the newspaper on the table, drank the rest of the port that remained in his glass and stood up.

Hans Wildau heard his phone ring and as he knew who could talk to him he sat on the bed and took the call immediately.

"*Ja, Herr Direktor.*"

"Hans, I must be brief. Things are unexpectedly getting extremely complicated here. Although I do not think they can get to me, I'm going to come out of the surface for a while. I'm leaving New York right now. I have a place in the woods where nobody will look for me. I have told Frau Schmiddel not to appear in the office anymore and to make a long trip of tourism that will be financed by us. Today I will close the office and I will keep it so until I have security guarantees again. I ask the same to you. I do not want you to run unnecessary dangers as a result of your return. Is there some place you can stay in China for a while?"

Wildau was a weather-beaten man because of the dangers and sudden storm fronts, so he answered without hesitation.

"Yes, *Herr Direktor*, I can stay in China without problems."

"Good Hans. I will contact you when the storm has passed. Now I must hang up."

"Very well, *Herr Direktor*. Good luck."

The Director could not guess the smile that appeared on his subordinate's lips. Wildau ran his hands over Liu Daiyu's long legs as she was lying on the bed with him and finally kissed her knees.

"My boss has always worried about his subordinates. He has asked me not to return home and to remain in China."

"The best news they could give me." Joyfully said the woman.

The meeting was scheduled for 5 p.m. and all the guests had arrived on time except Dr. Taro Suzuki, whose plane had delayed his departure due to a storm in the Pacific Ocean. All the expedition members were sitting alternately with the members of Bluthund's General Assembly, even those who were not members of the virtual community, such as Dieter von Eichenberg and Maggie Garland.

Dr. Richardson opened the session recalling that the expedition to Tibet had an antecedent a previous trip to Mongolia, in which it had found the remnants of the treasure of a kingdom in that nation that had existed briefly until the restoration of the republic. The tracks had then pointed to Tibet so that Bluthund had sponsored another expedition formed by the same members of the previous one, with some exceptions. The results of this second expedition had been advanced to the members of the General Assembly of the Community in a very diffuse way to avoid leaks of the information, but now they would have the opportunity to listen to the complete story with abundant documentary material, directly from the participants themselves.

Richardson gave the floor to Jack Berglund, founding partner of Bluthund and known by most of the attendees

At that moment two taps were heard at the door of the spacious room and Dr. Taro Suzuki entered, visibly dismayed by the delay. Richardson and Countess Nadia Swarowska approached the door to effusively greet their old friend and the meeting proceeded according to its schedule.

Berglund explained in detail the course of the trip, silencing however the coordinates of the sites of the findings, both that of the first cave and that of the second. With the help of Dennis he projected the important photographic and film material obtained, stopping in particular at the imposing marble tomb, which he estimated was of five and a half feet high. The inscriptions on the cover deserved a careful analysis and the debate was opened on that point.

"For what we may have observed the construction of the mausoleum does not correspond to Eastern architectural patterns but are clearly European." Said Dr. Suzuki. "On the other hand the swastika that we have seen is not the typical millennial oriental icon whose blades rotate in the reverse sense. It is without a doubt the Nazi symbol."

" I wonder what does it mean the phrase that whoever lies there will join his ancestors, as more or less reads the legend recorded also on the mausoleum." Asked one of the youngest attendees.

"It undoubtedly refers to the old Nazi theory of the development of the Aryan race in that area, belief that gave rise to a controversial expedition to Tibet by a scientist named Ernst Schäffer in 1938." Dieter said." I am aware of the veracity of the fact because my paternal grandfather was part of it, in the course of which he met my grandmother."

The debate continued for hours. One of the assistants asked.

" Since they had different purposes, what is the link between the expeditions to Mongolia and Tibet?"

Dennis hurried to answer.

"Good question. The thin red thread between them is the diary of the Russian Baron Roman Ungern von Sternberg, rescued by us in the first expedition to Mongolia, site where the Baron had acted, and in which he mentioned the location of the cave in Tibet."

" You mean that without finding of that diary or notebook the second expedition would not have been carried out?" Asked the young man.

"That´s right."

" So this finding has been subject to ... let's say ... small contingencies or coincidences. The results have been very random."

"It's true." answered Jack. "Many very important things sometimes depend on improbable or seemingly inconsequential events. One of the best examples is the reason why we succeeded in finding the crypt where our rivals did not."

"What was that reason?"

" That against our advice at a certain moment the young Martín Colombo decided to dive into the cold waters of the inner lake and thus found, by chance, the room where the mausoleum is located. Evidently our rivals did not have that same dangerous experience."

Another attendee decided to drastically change the subject.

" Who were part of the opposition? That is, who were your persecutors?"

At that moment Richardson resumed the floor.

"It is an international organization, just like ours but with opposite purposes. It is made up of old and new Nazis from almost all European countries, the United States, Turkey and other nations. As far as we know, they do not have a name and we do not know their leaders, but they have material and human resources superior to those of the Bluthund Community, no doubt due to their links with companies of originally Nazi capitals that were able to circumvent the filters imposed by the allies after the end of the Second World War."

"How did you find out that these people followed your steps?"

Suzuki took the floor.

"Our agents in Mongolia noticed unexpected activities and soon we could associate them with our expedition. Already alerted of their actions we were able to track them also in Tibet."

" So they followed us and we followed them. A circular chase."

"And quite a frequent one." answered Suzuki. "These are tasks of intelligence and counterintelligence. The important thing is to receive the original information of who is doing what in a given context."

Another attendee changed the subject again.

"How did they obtain information about our expeditions in the first place?"

"I sadly have to admit that it was due to a leak from one of our executives." answered abruptly Richardson. A murmur ran through the long table.

"Do you know who was the author of the leaks?" Tasked then the assistant

"Yes."

"And what happened to him?

"He's ... neutralized." answered briefly Richardson.

"In the army a neutralized enemy is a dead enemy." Argued a retired colonel.

"This is not the case."

"If it is not violating confidentiality, can I ask how could you detect the mole, that is, the one that caused the leak?"

Jack looked questioningly at Richardson who nodded.

"Because of the level of information the enemies had, there were two possible candidates for the role of traitor. After we determined the site of the true find, Maggie Garland, Dieter von Eichenberg and I meditated on the way to discover him. To each one of the candidates we provided different information about the coordinates of the finding."

"What information?"

"To one of them we gave the location of the tunnel that ended in an internal lake in the mountain, behind which we could not continue exploring due to a landslide in the past. We gave the other candidate other coordinates provided by Baron von Ungern's diary referring to another unrelated topic."

Jack looked at Suzuki, hoping he would go on with the explanation.

"With our contacts in China, we were able to determine which of the two false leads our rivals came to. When the persecutors moved towards the lake tunnel, the mole was exposed."

" Can we know his or her identity?"

Maggie came to the crossroads of this question.

"I will not reveal the identity of the traitor at this point. I will only tell you that he is a person who was linked to the English secret services in the past."

"A member of the Bluthund Community?"

"Yes." answered Richardson. "And even one of the founders and member of the Executive Committee, despite the fact that because of his age he was not a regular visitor."

Several of the attendees tied capes and drew the identity of the traitor.

The young man asked a spicy question.

" And who was the other candidate for a traitor, who in the end was innocent?"

Without hesitation William Richardson exclaimed.

"I!"

The murmur in the room grew louder. Suzuki took the floor again.

" Who was finally traitor on the one hand and Dr. Richardson on the other were the natural candidates because they were the two who had all the information. We would never have suspected any of them otherwise. When Jack Berglund called me from Tibet we decided to put the trap as explained."

Then he turned to Richardson and said.

"I'm sorry William, we have never suspected you, but the situation demanded that we make this move to clean your name."

"Of course Taro. In your place I would have done the same. What still bothers me is that it was the same traitor who warned me about the existence of a mole inside the Bluthund Community."

"He simply anticipated the conclusion that you would inevitably draw when the persecutors appeared in Tibet."Argued Madame Swarowska.

"You're right. Thank you dear. I had not thought about that." Richardson acknowledged.

The questions eventually ran out and at a certain moment Taro Suzuki said.

"I make a motion to entrust the Executive Committee to decide what we are going to do with the information obtained that is, whether to make it public or not. For this purpose, I propose that this Assembly make a recess and allow the Executive Committee to hold a meeting to make some decisions and then, after restarting the session of the Assembly, inform all its members on that decision."

The motion was put to a vote and approved unanimously. Richardson got up from his chair and said loudly.

"Before the Assembly enters in recess, I will make two additional proposals. The first is the following: as one of its members has been exposed as a traitor, I propose that the Executive Committee be entrusted to discharge him with dishonor. " He said referring to the master of ceremonies Jerome Watkins." Please. Proceed to the vote."

The proposal was voted unanimously once again. Richardson then said.

" My second proposal is that Jack Berglund be chosen to replace the traitor as a member of the Executive Committee. The appointment of the members of the Committee is a prerogative of this Assembly. I request that the members of the expedition first vacate the room, and then the master of ceremonies will proceed to distribute the ballots among the members of the Assembly. The election is made anonymously and as we know a single black ballot rejects the proposal."

Then the attendees who were not part of the Assembly left and the members proceeded to the vote.

The master of ceremonies made the recount and quickly announced the result.

"In this case it has been easy. All white ballots Jack Berglund is the new member of the Executive Committee."

Watkins called all the attendees who were located in several adjoining rooms.

"The Executive Committee has already made the decisions that were entrusted to it. Please return to the meeting room for the announcements."

Once everyone was seated William Richardson stood up and said.

"I inform you in the first place that the traitor in our midst was Sir David Osborne and that he has been expelled from the Bluthund Community with dishonor. His name will be deleted from all records where it once was."

A murmur of assent ran through the room.

"In the second place, the Committee has decided that the nature and location of the discovery will not be divulged due to its possible disastrous consequences for world politics. What international society needs least is a new and powerful factor of disunity. We know well that this decision is debatable because in some way it restricts the freedom of information but we believe that at present there are not yet the conditions for such a news to transcend."

In a private meeting between the members of the expedition, Jack Berglund received congratulations for his new and well-deserved position.

"The only thing you need to do now is to reconcile with your girlfriend." said Dennis with the familiarity that the shared adventures had given him with Berglund." What´s her name?"

"Lakshmi. Lakshmi Dhawan."

"Have you talked to her yet?"

"Yes, a couple of days ago."

"So?"

"We had already made peace earlier. I kept myself aloof because of the dangers I could expose to her and her daughter due to my enemies, as well as compromising her status as an FBI agent because of my ex convict status."

"And how are those issues now?"

"The ones that stalked me were precisely those who persecuted us in Tibet, those who now, although they have not disappeared, have had to step aside. And it seems that the FBI has received good references from our group and from my person in particular."

"And at what point are you now with her?"

"I'm going to meet Lakshmi these days to see how we can revive our relationship."

After this confession Jack added.

"As from now on all of us will return to their countries and to their activities, I would like us to have the opportunity to celebrate our fellowship together, without fears or shadows."

" Good! " Debbie exclaimed festively " Are you going to invite us to an exclusive French or Italian restaurant?"

"As you know, the position of member of the Executive Committee is ad honorem and has no associated stipends, so I invite you to close this chapter in the same way that we began months ago."

"That is?"

"With a picnic in the Bear Mountain Park."

And so, dear reader, this story has come to its end. But fear not, for new adventures await on the horizon, and the journey continues in the pages of tomorrow.

From the Author

Dear reader
I appreciate your interest in reading these few words in which I talk about my work. It is a good habit to try to understand what led an author to write a particular book, because the motivations vary from author to author and from book to book.

As a sign of respect for the reader, in all my books I make a thorough previous investigation of the facts the work refers to, particularly considering that many of them take place in places sometimes very far apart from each other and also in various historical periods; my books often travel indeed through dilated stretches in time and space.

These searches are based on my memory, in the large family library and the huge quarry of facts and data existing in the Internet. In the global network everyone can search but not all find the same ... fortunately, since these results in a huge variability and diversity.

The plot of course comes from the imagination and fantasy. This is critical for me and I confess that I would never write a book that I wouldn´t like to read; my interests as a writer and as a reader coincide to a large degree.

My works often take place in exotic locations and refer sometimes to surprising and even paradoxical facts, but never enter the realm of the fantastic and incredible. Moreover, the most bizarre events are often true.

About the Author

Cedric Daurio is the pen name an Argentine novelist uses for certain types of narrative, in general thrillers with esoteric or paranormal content. The author has lived in New York for years and now resides in Buenos Aires, his hometown. His style is clear and straightforward, and does not hesitate to tackle thorny issues.

Works by Cedric Daurio

In English
Blood Runes
The Agartha Star
(Both novels are included in the Bluthund Community series)

En Spanish
Runas de Sangre

La Estrella de Agartha

(Both novels are included in the Comunidad Bluthund series)

Coordinates of the Author

Mailto: cedricdaurio@gmail.com
Blog: https://cedricdauriobooks.wordpress.com/blog/

About the Publisher

Oscar Luis Rigiroli publishes the books in print and electronic editions through a commercial network that provides them with an ample worldwide coverage including sales in the five continents. The catalog includes titles of its own authorship as those written by other authors. All works are available in Spanish and English.

Abundant information on these titles can be consulted in the following websites:

Https://narrativaoscarrigiroli.wordpress.com/

and

Https://louisforestiernarrativa.wordpress.com/[1]

THE READER IS KINDLY invited to consult them in the certainty of finding good reading experiences.

---

1. https://louisforestiernarrativa.wordpress.com/

Milton Keynes UK
Ingram Content Group UK Ltd.
UKHW040809051024
449151UK00001B/70